P9-DXM-311

Despite his attempt to block them, images of Grace Chancellor had been bombarding his brain since Dalton had mentioned her name. Memories of the woman he had first met…almost ten years ago, he realized with a sense of wonder.

Grace Chancellor and Afghanistan. Two items of unfinished—and very personal—business.

Landon hadn't made many mistakes since the years he'd been an operative. In his line of work he couldn't afford them. What Cabot had set forth before him this morning was a chance to rectify the two most spectacular ones he'd made in his entire life. If Grace was alive, he'd find her. And if she wasn't… Landon took a deep breath, thinking about what that loss would mean.

"Hang on, Gracie," he whispered. "The bastards haven't won one yet. They damn sure aren't going to win this time, either."

Dear Harlequin Intrigue Reader,

This July, Intrigue brings you six sizzling summer reads. They're the perfect beach accessory.

* We have three fantastic miniseries for you. *Film at Eleven* continues THE LANDRY BROTHERS by Kelsey Roberts. Gayle Wilson is back with the PHOENIX BROTHERHOOD in *Take No Prisoners*. And B.J. Daniels finishes up her McCALLS' MONTANA series with *Shotgun Surrender*.

* Susan Peterson brings you *Hard Evidence*, the final installment in our LIPSTICK LTD. promotion featuring stealthy sleuths. And, of course, we have a spine-tingling ECLIPSE title. This month's is Patricia Rosemoor's *Ghost Horse*.

* Don't miss Dana Marton's sexy stand-alone title, *The Sheik's Safety*. When an American soldier is caught behind enemy lines, she'll fake amnesia to guard her safety, but there's no stopping the sheik determined on winning her heart.

Enjoy our stellar lineup this month and every month!

Sincerely,

Denise O'Sullivan
Senior Editor
Harlequin Intrigue

TAKE NO PRISONERS

GAYLE WILSON

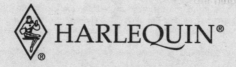

HARLEQUIN®

TORONTO • NEW YORK • LONDON
AMSTERDAM • PARIS • SYDNEY • HAMBURG
STOCKHOLM • ATHENS • TOKYO • MILAN • MADRID
PRAGUE • WARSAW • BUDAPEST • AUCKLAND

For the guys and gals of my RWA chapter, Southern Magic. Thank you for your support and most of all for your friendship. You'll never know how much you mean to me.

ISBN 0-373-22856-2

TAKE NO PRISONERS

Copyright © 2005 by Mona Gay Thomas

This edition published by arrangement with Harlequin Books S.A.

www.eHarlequin.com

Printed in U.S.A.

ABOUT THE AUTHOR

Five-time RITA® Award finalist and RITA® Award winner Gayle Wilson has written over thirty novels and three novellas for Harlequin/Silhouette. She has won more than forty awards and nominations for her work.

Gayle still lives in Alabama, where she was born, with her husband of thirty-four years. She loves to hear from readers. Write to her at P.O. Box 3277, Hueytown, AL 35023. Visit Gayle online at www.booksbygaylewilson.com.

Books by Gayle Wilson

CAST OF CHARACTERS

Landon James—The only woman this ex-CIA agent has ever loved is being held captive in the mountains of Afghanistan. There is no question he'll go after her. The only question is whether he can find her in time.

Grace Chancellor—She had risen quickly in the ranks of the CIA, but her fall has been even more spectacular. Now her life hangs in the balance. And the one person who has the skills to rescue her is the man she walked away from six years ago.

Griff Cabot—The leader of the Phoenix is willing to go outside his own organization if necessary to save Grace Chancellor's life.

Mike Mitchell—Taken prisoner with Grace, the dying pilot teaches her a lesson that would change her life.

Rudolph Stern—Grace refuses to abandon her fellow prisoner, despite the price she may pay for her loyalty.

Abdul Rahim—No one is more eager for Landon James's return to Afghanistan than this drug lord with a long memory and a thirst for revenge.

Steven Reynolds—Will this Special Forces operative drive a wedge between Landon and Grace? Or is it possible Landon isn't the only one guarding secrets?

Prologue

"The heroin is taken out of the country by routes established centuries ago. Most of it goes through Tajikistan or Uzbekistan and on to Russia and China."

Despite the noise of the Kiowa's jet engine, Colonel Rudolph Stern seemed determined to keep up the ongoing dialogue he'd begun as soon as he met Grace Chancellor's car at his headquarters. In the close confines of the chopper, he was leaning against her, practically shouting in her ear.

Of course, Grace had been well aware of almost all the information he'd provided long before she'd left Langley. In spite of that, she nodded, having decided a couple of hours ago that the occasional gesture of agreement was the easiest way to deal with her gregarious military host.

It had been painfully obvious from the first he didn't believe she was the right person for the job she'd been given. Just as obviously, he didn't realize that his attitude was nothing new.

Grace had spent more than a decade climbing the

ranks in the CIA, an agency that celebrated its old-boys network. And Grace Chancellor had never been one of the "old boys."

"In spite of our presence here," Stern went on, "massive shipments still make it though those mountains and into Pakistan." He nodded toward the chopper's open door and the rugged peaks that stretched below.

This trip along the Afghan/Pakistani border had been an afterthought. Stern had already shown her the vast fields of poppies that now covered the relatively fertile valleys of Afghanistan. In full bloom, their flowers had thrown a blaze of color across the otherwise monochromatic landscape.

With the disruption of the Taliban's control, the country's trade in heroin had once again grown to staggering proportions. More than one-fifth of the world's opium was currently being produced here.

Although heavily backed by an American and British commitment of money and manpower, recent attempts by the Afghan government to rein in that very profitable business had led to deep resentment and even violence among the general population. In a country whose grinding poverty rivaled any in the region, people were dependent on the cash produced by the poppies to feed their children.

It was now Grace's job to find a workable solution for all of those involved. And to do it before the antipathy generated by the attempts to control the drug trafficking boiled over into a full-blown rebellion.

No one at the CIA, including Grace herself, had had any doubt that her current assignment was a demotion.

In her opinion at least, it had been intended as a punishment, as well, but she was determined that the people at the Agency who had made this decision would never have the satisfaction of hearing her complain.

Almost the only thing she could control in this situation was how she conducted herself. Despite her bitterness over the undeserved castigation, she was resolute in her intent to bring to this challenge the same degree of professionalism and all-out effort she had invested in everything else the Agency had ever asked of her.

The colonel, a tall, spare man already deeply tanned by the relentless Afghan sun, raised his index finger and then moved it in a circle. His aide, who had apparently been keeping a watchful eye on their conversation, placed his hand on the shoulder of the chopper pilot and bent to shout whatever unspoken instruction he'd just been given against his flight helmet. The helicopter immediately began to turn, its nose tilting slightly downward as it did.

Before it had completed the maneuver, there was a loud bang. The Kiowa seemed to hesitate in midair, almost as if it were catching its breath.

Then the noise of the jet engine, which had made normal conversation impossible, was no longer there. In its sudden and eerie absence Grace could hear what sounded like the clatter of small-arms fire from below and the continuing *whomp, whomp, whomp* of the rotor blades over their heads.

"What the hell?" Stern muttered before he leaned forward, shouting the same question to his aide.

As he did, Grace was again able see the ground beneath the chopper. Following the Kiowa's shadow, a stream of horsemen galloped over the rocky terrain below. The gunfire she'd heard had obviously come from the rifles they brandished in upraised hands.

She couldn't hear the answer the aide had conveyed from the pilot to Stern, but the colonel's expression when he turned toward her left no doubt that it hadn't been what he'd been hoping to hear. His lips flattened as she met his eyes, trying to keep hers from revealing the fear that had already tightened her chest and rested cold and queasy in the bottom of her stomach.

"Looks like the bastards got lucky."

Unlike the colonel's previous comments, this one hadn't been shouted. And there was a note in his voice she liked even less than she had liked his previous condescending manner.

"What does that mean?"

The hesitation before he answered lasted through several more endless seconds. Her heart rate, already elevated, increased exponentially while she waited.

"They hit the engine with those pea shooters. We're going down."

His eyes held hers, watching for reaction, she supposed. Although she tried to control any outward sign of what she was feeling, she was the one who finally broke the contact between them, looking down again on the horsemen who, even as she watched, seemed to grow larger and more menacing. The pilot fought to control their too-rapid descent, the blades thankfully still turning above their heads, allowing him a chance to try to set the chopper down.

She'd always heard that when you faced death, your entire life flashed before your eyes. Fingers tense around the metal arms of her seat, she realized that in her case, at least, that wasn't true. There was only one image that kept repeating over and over in her head.

She had run into one of the old hands at the Agency shortly after she'd been called to testify before Congress. She hadn't seen him in a couple of years, certainly not to talk to, so that she'd wondered at the time if he had arranged their "chance" meeting. If so, she was grateful. Most of the others at Langley had simply turned the other way as she walked by.

Neil Andrews had looked her in the eye. His warning had been equally straight and to the point:

"Watch your back," he'd said. "Don't think for a minute that they're going to let you get away with it."

"I'm sorry," Stern said, bringing her abruptly back to the present. He sounded as if he might actually mean it.

Of course he does, she told herself. To believe anything else was sheer paranoia. After all, whatever dangers lay ahead, the colonel and his aide would experience them, as well.

Except they aren't women, Grace acknowledged, looking down again on the barren ground and the riders who seemed to be rising up to meet their rapid descent. And although she had functioned in a masculine realm for years, she knew with a cold certainty that the world she was about encounter was far different in its approach to women than any she had ever faced before.

Chapter One

"I've already told Griff I'm not interested. Several times, actually."

The deep voice on the other end of the line seemed resigned, almost amused rather than angry. Dalton Rawls knew that amusement wouldn't last.

This was a call he'd been dreading having to make for several days, ever since Griff Cabot had broached the idea. They had both agreed, however, that there was no one better suited for this mission than Landon James. And since technically it wasn't a Phoenix undertaking...

"This isn't about joining the Phoenix," Dalton said.

There was a beat of silence as the ex-CIA operative he'd just phoned digested the information. "Then what is it about?"

"A mutual acquaintance who's in trouble."

The silence this time was even more prolonged.

"If this isn't about the Phoenix, then I suppose I should assume that whoever we're talking about wasn't part of the External Security Team, either."

Griff Cabot's elite counterterrorism unit had been

destroyed by the Agency long before the terrorist attack that had devastated the heart of the country. The Phoenix, a private investigative agency, had been born from the EST's ashes. Although Landon James had been a member of the CIA team from its inception, he had refused every inducement to join the private group of agents Cabot had put together during the last five years, its members almost exclusively drawn from his former operatives.

"We're talking about Grace Chancellor," Dalton said, seeing no point in making a mystery of his request. "Griff said you'd remember her."

The quality of the silence this time was different somehow. As ridiculous as it seemed to believe he could judge something like that over the phone, Dalton knew he'd just taken the other man by surprise. A feat that had once been almost impossible to achieve.

"I remember."

Dalton couldn't quite read the tone of those two words, but he'd been right in his earlier speculation. Both the resignation *and* the amusement had disappeared.

"Tell me," Landon demanded into his continued silence.

"You know that she testified before Congress a few months ago."

"You mean when she told the Hill that their vaunted intelligence services—all of them—didn't know what the hell they were doing during one of the most critical periods in this nation's history?"

"I don't believe she phrased it in exactly that way," Dalton said, making no effort to conceal his own amusement at how accurately Landon's opinion echoed those that had been expressed privately among the members of the Phoenix.

The destruction of the EST had been only one of the many intelligence blunders made by those in authority during the last ten years, but it had been the most personal for all of them. Certainly the most bitter. At least until New York.

Eventually both the country and Congress had begun to ask why no one had been aware of the threat from Al-Qaeda. Maybe, Dalton thought, because they'd all been too busy getting rid of the very people who might have been able to tell them. And that would certainly have included Landon James.

The Middle East had been his area of expertise. Just as it was Grace Chancellor's. She'd been an intelligence analyst rather than an operative, but despite the fact that the two had struck sparks off one another on a number of occasions by supporting conflicting opinions about operations there, Dalton knew Landon had respected her opinions.

Whether that respect would translate into the ex-CIA agent taking action in this situation was something neither he nor Griff had been willing to predict. Neither had they been willing to bet against it.

If Landon refused, then Griff would move on to Plan B. With Cabot there was *always* a Plan B. They had agreed, however, that Landon James was their best hope.

And Grace Chancellor's best hope, as well.

"Apparently she phrased it strongly enough that it's

gotten her into trouble," Landon said. "I'm just not sure what you expect me to do about it."

"I don't believe the trouble she's in right now can be blamed entirely on her testimony," Dalton said carefully.

He didn't want to suggest too much, but he also knew that the only chance he had of convincing James to undertake this mission was to be absolutely straight with him. Landon was too perceptive not to recognize when he was being played.

"The company despises whistle blowers," Landon said. "Even those compelled to testify under oath."

"So much so," Dalton agreed, "that as a result of her testimony, the powers-that-be found Chancellor a new assignment."

"Let me guess. Reading satellite images."

"Something slightly more challenging." Despite the seriousness of the situation, Dalton found himself smiling at the reminder of how hated that particular assignment was among Cabot's agents. "They put her in charge of stopping the heroin traffic out of Afghanistan."

Landon laughed, the sound short and harsh. "I'm surprised they didn't give her a spoon and a bucket and point her toward the nearest ocean."

Again Landon was on target with his assessment of the task Chancellor had been given. Halting the exportation of heroin from Afghanistan was an impossible job, considering the entrenched culture of poppy production. It had been made even more difficult now by the lawlessness of the vast areas that lay outside the direct control of the Afghan government or the forces of the international coalition.

"Chancellor wanted to see the extent of the problem for herself," Dalton went on, "as well as every aspect of the process by which the drugs are transported out of the country."

There was a noise from the other end of the line that sounded like derision. Unsure, Dalton decided to ignore it.

"The Army provided her with a military escort, some lieutenant colonel who was supposed to know the ropes and show her around. Chancellor probably knew more about what was going on before she arrived in the country than he did after several months there."

"And knowing Chancellor," Landon said, "she didn't tell him that."

Probably not, Dalton thought, but he ignored the interruption to go on with his story. "The Kiowa they were riding in was hit by small-arms fire. Fortunately the pilot was able to set the chopper down, but…"

"Go on," Landon urged when Dalton paused.

The voice on the other end of the line had become very soft. It was a timbre anyone who had worked in the field with Landon James would have recognized immediately. The more tense the situation, the quieter he became.

"The body of the colonel's aide was found with the helicopter. Lt. Colonel Stern, the pilot and Grace Chancellor were not."

"Where did they go down?"

"The mountains just north of Kabul."

"Son of a bitch." The expletive was again soft, but obviously heartfelt. "How long ago?"

This was the part Dalton had most dreaded. So far the Agency had been tight-lipped about the incident. There had been a brief report in the media, no names provided. If Neil Andrews hadn't contacted Griff, they might never have known Grace was involved.

"Nearly two weeks."

The expletive Landon uttered this time was expressive of his contempt. "And of course, no one at Langley has a clue who took them. Or where."

Those were not questions. They were assumptions, flatly articulated and based on Landon's lack of respect for the kind of information gathering that had passed for intel in that area for years.

"Not a clue. At least, according to Griff's sources within the Agency."

"Griff wants me to find her?"

The hesitation this time was Dalton's. "He recognizes that he has no right to ask you to do anything. He simply wanted me to make you aware of what had happened."

"Okay," Landon said. "Tell him I'm aware."

Which didn't sound promising. Nor did it reveal what the ex-operative intended to do. If anything.

Dalton suspected his boss wasn't going to be satisfied if he brought back that enigmatic answer. He knew Griff well enough to know that if James didn't accept the task, Cabot would find someone who would.

His loyalty toward those he considered the good guys within the CIA extended beyond the agents who had worked for him. Apparently, it covered Grace Chancellor, as well. And Griff would damn well want to know if the rescue mission he'd been hoping for was going to take place.

"*Are* you going to find her?" Dalton asked.

"If she's still alive."

"We have no reason to believe she isn't."

And none to believe she is.

"Anybody had an offer?"

"For ransom, you mean?"

"Someone in that region is holding a senior CIA analyst, an American colonel and an American pilot, and they aren't trying to negotiate a deal for their release? Doesn't that strike you as strange?"

"It's a pretty remote area. A lot of tribesmen—"

"You just made the same kind of mistake our former employer so frequently makes," Landon interrupted. "Don't judge sophistication by lifestyle. Just because someone lives in a cave doesn't mean he doesn't know what's going on in the outside world. That should have been one lesson we all learned from 9/11."

"Then…why wouldn't anyone have been approached for ransom?"

"I don't know, but I can tell you that single fact bothers me more than anything else you've told me."

Dalton swallowed his own misgivings over the way the capture of the three Americans had played out reinforced by Landon's certainty that something was wrong with the entire scenario.

"Someone mentioned the possibility that this has been organized by the drug lords," he said. "Something designed to show that no matter how many people Washington sends out, they're still in control."

"If there's to be any chance of Grace Chancellor being returned alive, you better hope whoever told you that is wrong."

Dalton had no idea what to say to that. It sounded ominous. And absolutely assured.

"I still don't know what you want me to tell Griff."

"Tell him I don't work for him anymore."

"Believe me, he knows that, Landon."

"Does he?" James asked, the hint of amusement Dalton had heard at the beginning of the conversation back in his voice. "And yet, strangely enough, this conversation sounds exactly like those he used to employ to get me interested in whatever he wanted me interested in during the External Security Team days."

"Are you? Interested, I mean?"

"I'm a few years older and light-years wiser than I was when I worked for the CIA."

"I don't believe you've changed that much."

Although Dalton had probably been the closest thing to a friend Landon James had had on the EST, he hadn't seen his fellow operative in years. At Cabot's request, he'd made the occasional contact to try to recruit him on the Phoenix's behalf, only to be turned down each time.

He had no idea what Landon was doing right now. Griff probably knew, but he hadn't passed on that information along with James's phone number.

"Apparently not enough that Griff can't manage to hit all the right buttons."

"I don't think that's what he's trying to do. I think he just hoped that since this is your area of expertise…"

"I'd ride to the rescue."

"With all your expenses paid by the Phoenix, of course."

"Paid on whose behalf?"

The Phoenix was very much a "for-hire" operation, although their charges were usually dependent on the client's ability to pay. More than a few missions were undertaken on a pro bono basis, however, especially if Cabot felt that justice could be achieved only through their intervention.

"I don't believe Grace has any family—" Dalton began, only to be cut off in midsentence.

"She doesn't. I suspect our illustrious leader will be footing the bill himself. Not that he can't afford it."

Griff Cabot came from very old money. A lot of it. And James was right. He could afford to mount any quixotic rescue he believed should be undertaken.

"I don't think he's counting the cost on this one."

"No, Griff always did have a penchant for lost causes."

"Then… You think they're *dead*?"

"Actually, that wasn't what I meant at all."

The amusement was back, but Dalton had no idea what had caused it. Nor did he have a clue as to what James was talking about.

"I don't understand—" he began.

"It doesn't matter," Landon said briskly. "Tell Griff he pushed the right buttons this time. Obviously he hasn't lost the fine art of leadership."

"Then you're going after them?" Dalton couldn't keep the relief out of his voice.

"I'm going after Gracie. If the others are there, I'll try my best to get them out, too.

Gracie? In all the years Dalton had known Grace Chancellor, he had never heard anyone ever refer to her as Gracie. The nickname was totally foreign to the cool, collected persona the intelligence analyst exuded.

Or maybe, Dalton thought, as a click and then the dial tone reverberated in his ear, it was just that he didn't know Grace Chancellor nearly so well as Landon James did.

Something else Cabot had apparently failed to tell him.

LANDON JAMES PUT DOWN the phone and swiveled his desk chair around until he was looking out over the tops of some of the tallest buildings in New York. He'd been able to lease this office space high above the city for a song in the days immediately after the terrorist attack. No one, it seemed, had wanted to work in the clouds anymore.

After a moment he stood up and walked across the huge room to a wall of windows, thinking instead about the phone call he'd just concluded. Despite his attempt to block them, images of Grace Chancellor had flooded his brain since Dalton had mentioned her name. Memories of the woman he had first met almost…almost ten years ago, he realized with a sense of wonder.

He couldn't believe it had been that long. He should, he acknowledged. A lot had changed in that time.

Including him. Maybe *especially* him.

He realized that he was unconsciously fingering the patch that covered the empty socket of what had been his right eye. He forced his fingers away from it, his lips tightening as he remembered how that loss had occurred.

Grace Chancellor and Afghanistan. Two items of unfinished—and very personal—business.

There weren't many of either in his life these days. Other than the security consultation firm he'd started almost as soon as he resigned from the Agency, there was very little that touched him personally anymore. Both of those did.

Grace Chancellor and Afghanistan.

How well Griff knew him, he thought, his lips lifting in a smile of self-derision. And how cleverly he had chosen his weapons.

Landon hadn't made many mistakes in the years he'd been an operative. In his line of work, he couldn't afford them.

What Cabot had set before him this morning, like the food and water the ancient gods had set before Tantalus, was a chance to rectify the two most spectacular ones he'd made in his entire life. And to do it at Griff's expense.

That wasn't entirely true, he acknowledged, no matter what Dalton offered. Money was the least of what this journey would cost. And there was no guarantee that he would be able to do what the U.S. Special Forces in the area had not be able to accomplish and find the three Americans. That didn't mean he wasn't going to try.

If Grace was alive, he'd find her. And if she wasn't… He took a deep breath, thinking about what that loss would mean.

"Hang on, Gracie," he whispered, looking down on the area still marked by the attack of madmen. "The bastards haven't won one yet. They damn sure aren't going to win this time, either."

Chapter Two

"Better?"

Mike Mitchell opened fever-bright eyes to look up into hers. His cracked lips lifted in a ghastly semblance of a smile. "Thanks," he whispered.

Grace set down the cup of tepid water from which she'd just helped the pilot drink. She put her hand on his chest, wishing there was something else she could do to ease his suffering. Not that any complaints had crossed his lips in the weeks of their captivity.

Every day, however, she had watched a little more life slip out of those blue eyes. And every night she had listened to his labored breathing until she fell asleep, praying that she would still be able to hear it when she awoke.

"Try to get some rest," she said inanely.

The grin widened before it became a grimace. Mitchell closed his eyes against the wave of pain, but when he opened them, he smiled at her again.

"I didn't have anything much on my agenda for today."

"That's good," she said, returning the smile, despite her fury at their captors.

Although she and Colonel Stern had begged for a doctor to see the pilot or for some kind of exchange to be made that would put him in the hands of either the coalition forces or the International Red Cross, their entreaties had been met with stony-eyed indifference. And with each day of their captivity, Mitchell had lost ground.

The infection that could have, at one time at least, been easily treated with antibiotics now ran rampant throughout his wasted body. If something didn't change soon…

She turned away, trying to pretend that she'd been distracted by a noise outside the cave. In reality she needed a moment to regain control of her emotions. And she didn't intend for Mike to see her tears.

Actually, she didn't intend to shed any, she decided, fighting the burn at the back of her eyes. She had always despised crying women.

She hadn't broken down when the Agency had "disciplined" her. Or in those first few terrifying hours after the crash. She wasn't going to do it now. Not in front of a man who had kept his sense of humor and his will to live intact, despite the battle of survival he had been fighting—and was now losing.

She recognized that the causes of her emotional vulnerability ran even deeper than her anger over Mike Mitchell's treatment. There was also the gnawing uncertainty about what was going to happen to them, as well as the frustration of having no control over whatever did.

Despite Stern's insistence that they be afforded the same protections given prisoners of war—an insistence that had earned him the butt of a rifle in his stomach the last time he'd made it—the conditions under which they were kept had been both primitive and deliberately intimidating. Her immediate fear that she might be subject to sexual assault had thankfully not proven true.

Of course, neither had her hope that the men who held them would ransom them to some of the friendly forces in the area come to fruition. And again, frustratingly, she knew that those forces were very close.

For one thing, they had been moved three times in as many weeks. In the distance behind them they had heard both small-arms fire and the sounds of heavy bombardment. Not surprisingly, considering what she knew about the reliability of U.S. humint in the region, their captors seemed to have better information than whoever was searching for them.

Please God, let them still be searching for us...

Mitchell's hand, almost skeletal now, closed over hers. She turned back, looking down at him.

He was lying on a rough pallet of rugs and blankets, which were all they'd been provided in the way of bedding. Despite the cold mountain nights, she and the colonel had given most of their share of those to keep Mitchell as warm and comfortable as possible, even as the relentless infection spread from the bullet hole in his thigh throughout his body.

She should have known what kind of treatment they were in for when one of the horsemen who had surrounded the downed chopper shot the pilot as he'd climbed out of the cockpit, his hands in the air. Stern's aide had reacted by going for the weapon he'd already thrown down. He had died in the attempt.

"It's going to be okay," Mike said.

She smiled at him in response, refusing to comment on that ridiculous promise.

"You got somebody, Grace?"

"What?"

"Somebody who's waiting for you back home."

Mitchell had already shown her pictures of his wife and two children, a little girl almost three and a six-month-old baby boy. She couldn't begin to imagine what these weeks must have been like for them. And for Mike, of course, thinking about what their life would be without him.

"Not really," she said.

"You should have."

"I guess I've been too busy with other things," she said, a trace of defensiveness creeping into her voice.

"Lying here like this… Thinking about it all…" He attempted a laugh, which turned into a cough. "I guess this sounds stupid, but lying here, I've been thinking about life. You know?"

Life *and* death. How well she knew.

"And what earth-shattering conclusions have you come to?"

She dipped the piece of cloth she'd torn from one of the blankets into the bucket of water at the head of his pallet. She used the rag to bathe his face, although by this late in the day, the temperature of the water she'd been allowed to bring inside the cave was almost as hot as the surrounding air. Still, it was cooler than the brow of the man who was literally burning up before her eyes.

"That it's all that matters."

"I'm sorry?"

Her attention had been momentarily distracted by the dry heat of his skin. It seemed hotter this afternoon than she had ever felt it before.

And she realized belatedly that it had been more than twelve hours since Mike had asked Stern to help him urinate. She wasn't sure what that meant medically, but obviously it wasn't anything good.

"Having somebody to love you. Somebody you love in return. It's the only thing that matters."

With her heart breaking for the young wife and children who had loved this good, strong man, she smiled at him, once more fighting the sting of tears.

"I need to work on that," she said, squeezing the water out of the cloth and preparing to lay it over his forehead.

His hand lifted, grasping her wrist before she could. "I *mean* it."

"I know. I know you do. It's just that… Not all of us are as lucky as you and Karen. Some of us…" She hesitated, trying to find words to describe the long-ago decision that had left her so alone. "Either we don't find the right person to share our lives with or they don't feel the same way about us that we feel about them."

"Is that what happened to you?"

Her immediate instinct was to lie. To cover up the heartbreak she'd never forgotten. The one she'd tried to bury in hard work and furthering her career.

Mike Mitchell deserved better than that from her. Besides, what in the world could it matter what she told him? They were never going to get out of here.

At least...*he* wasn't.

"Yeah," she said, turning her wrist gently to break his fragile hold. "That's what happened to me."

She laid the cloth on his forehead and then leaned back to meet his eyes. Despite the situation, his were filled with compassion.

"How long ago?"

"Too long. Way too long."

"And there hasn't been anyone else?"

"He was a pretty tough act to follow," she said, smiling at him with lips that felt numb.

What the hell was she doing sitting in a cave in Afghanistan discussing Landon James with a dying man? Was this what her life had come down to?

"You ever try to contact him? Reconnect? I mean... People change. Maybe..."

Mike's shoulders moved in an approximation of a shrug, which was followed by a pained twisting of his face. This time a small expression of discomfort emerged from between the cracked lips.

"I don't think he would have, but no, I never contacted him."

"Maybe when you get out of here, I mean...maybe you ought to try to get in touch with him."

"Yeah. I think I'll do that. When pigs fly," she added, laughing a little at her stupid joke.

"What could it hurt?"

My pride. My self-image. My hard-earned sense of the completeness of my life as it is now.

Or my life as it was, she amended. *Before we ended up here.*

Yeah, things were damn good before you ended up here. That's why you came home every night with a stack of research material. Highly entertaining. Better than a lover any day of the week.

Better than a lover who had wanted to be nothing more.

And you always had to have it all. The brass ring. The whole nine yards. All those other clichés. You couldn't be satisfied with what Landon had to offer. All he had to offer.

"…just wish I'd said everything I felt."

She came out of her reverie to catch the last part of what Mike was saying. It was enough, however, to let her know exactly what he was thinking.

"You will." This time she acknowledged, to herself at least, the terrible lie that was. "Besides, even without the words, I think the people we love know how we feel about them."

But that wasn't good enough for you, was it? You had to have the words.

"God, I hope so," the pilot whispered.

She nodded, unwilling to trust her voice. For a long time neither of them said anything. The light faded from the entrance to the cave and with it the daytime warmth.

Night would fall quickly now. A cold, black eternity during which she would lie on the clammy rock floor, listening to the breathing of the man who, in these short weeks, had become a friend.

Listening also to the measured pace of the guard outside. To the noises of the encampment. The restless movement of the horses. The occasional unrestrained laughter of their captors.

Listening until it all faded like a familiar soundtrack

behind the images that would parade through her mind for hours as she slept. Landon's hands on her body. His mouth lowering to claim hers. His laughter, rare and far more precious for its rarity.

What would it hurt to try? Mike Mitchell had asked her.

Maybe it wouldn't, but she knew she couldn't take the chance. All she had to measure that risk by was how very much it had hurt before.

"They're planning to move us again," Stern announced from the doorway where he'd been watching the activity outside.

She glanced down at Mike to gauge his reaction and found his eyes closed, his breathing shallow but regular. It was just as well he hadn't heard, she decided as she got carefully to her feet, leaving the damp cloth lying across his brow. She didn't want to think what it would cost him to make another relocation. He had been measurably worse after the last.

"How do you know?" she whispered to Stern as she crossed to the entrance.

"They're packing. They aren't hurrying with it, and the cooking utensils are still out, so it won't be tonight. Probably tomorrow before dawn."

That had been the timing of the first two moves. The third had occurred shortly after midnight, a hurried scramble that had obviously been the result of some last-minute decision or threat.

"Do you think that means someone's located us?"

Without lifting his eyes from their contemplation of the camp, Stern said, "If we're lucky. Except that every time they do…"

She knew what he meant. Every time the people searching for them got close, they were moved. It was like a game of chess. Or like the children's game of hide-and-seek, with their captors knowing all the best hiding places.

Neither she nor Stern could figure out why they were still dragging the three of them around. The best-case scenario was that the men holding them were in the process of negotiating an exchange. The fact that they didn't appear to care if Mitchell died, however, seemed to counter that hopeful theory.

The worst case was probably that she and Stern were being offered for sale to someone, maybe Al-Qaeda, for whom they would have value as sources of information. In that situation, Mike would clearly be expendable.

"Maybe this time they'll find us."

And maybe pigs really will fly, she thought, negating her own comment.

After all, she was here because she had conveyed this exact reality to Congress: Human intelligence gathering in this region had been virtually nonexistent for years, and it was impossible to identify from satellite images what the people hiding in these caves were doing.

"I don't understand why they haven't mounted a larger-scale campaign to get us back," Stern said.

Maybe because you had the misfortune to get captured with me.

Grace had never expressed that feeling aloud, but her conviction—that the people in charge of "special activities" here had just as soon she never be found—had grown with each passing day. It would be a shame if

Stern and Mike were to be sacrificed because of her supposed sins, but there was very little she could do about it if that were the case. Not here. And not now.

"How is he?" Stern finally looked up, pulling his attention briefly from the flurry of activity outside.

"I think he's dying," Grace said softly.

"Then I hope to God he does it before morning."

GRACE HAD NO IDEA how long it had been since she'd lain down. Long enough that she was deeply asleep when the hand on her shoulder roughly shook her awake and short enough that it felt as if she'd had no rest at all.

She opened her eyes to find a man she'd never seen before stooping beside her. Although his mustache was coal black, it wasn't very full, almost as if he might recently have been clean shaven.

A patch covered his right eye. Glittering in the light from the dying fire, the remaining one seemed as cold and as black as the night.

He had said nothing, simply crouching beside her. Of course, he didn't need to issue instructions. By this time she knew the drill.

She shrugged her shoulder away, freeing it from the touch of his hand, and began to rise. He grabbed her arm, turning her toward him again.

She looked up in shock and found that he had one finger across his lips, the universal sign for silence. She nodded her understanding and immediately he released her.

As she began to roll up her blanket, he stood, the move accomplished in one smoothly athletic motion, and walked over to where Stern was wrapped in his own blanket, his back to the fire. Grace was surprised that the colonel, usually a light sleeper, hadn't already awakened, but then, the man moved virtually without sound across the floor of the cave.

He bent, touching Stern on the shoulder, just as he had her. The colonel rolled over, looking up at him in the dim firelight. Again the man put his finger over his lips.

He said something, his tone so low that Grace was unable to distinguish the words, although she had managed to pick up a little of their captors' dialect since the crash. In response to the man's comment, Stern pointed toward the heavily shadowed interior portion of the cave where Mitchell slept.

They had moved him there themselves that afternoon in an attempt to get him into a cooler area during the fierce heat of midday. Tonight they hadn't had the heart to try to move him back nearer the fire. They had simply piled the remaining blankets around him, despite the heat that emanated from his ravaged body.

Before the man who had awakened them went back to the pilot's pallet, he said something else to the colonel, who nodded. Grace watched as he walked by her, headed, she assumed, to arouse Mitchell.

"Come on. We have to get ready to go."

She turned to find Stern standing beside her, close enough that she had understood his whisper. She nodded, reaching down for the blanket she'd already rolled up.

"Leave it," the colonel said, taking her arm.

"But—"

"Shh…" he cautioned, drawing her across the cave

to the entrance where he crouched, pulling her down beside him.

It took Grace a second or two to realize why it seemed so eerily silent outside. The tread of the guard stationed at the entrance to the cave, so familiar it had become like the noise of her own heartbeat, was missing.

"Where's the—"

"Shh…" Stern whispered again.

She closed her mouth, considering the possible implications of his repeated warnings and the absence of the guard. The only logical conclusion for both—

"Let's go."

The man with the eye patch was back, standing behind them. That was her first realization. The second was that he had just whispered instructions to them in English.

English that had been spoken with an American accent.

"What about Mike?" she asked, looking up into a lean face that, partially lit by the dying fire, seemed as sinister as that of any of their captors.

"He's dead." The intonation of those two words had been flat. And final.

And they had not provided nearly enough information. "Are you sure?"

"Absolutely."

"It won't take but a minute—"

As she rose and attempted to move past him, the stranger grasped her arm, pulling her around so that he could grip shoulders. Although he never raised his voice above a whisper, each word he spoke was clear and distinct.

"You never did know to shut up and do what you're told, did you, Gracie? That's why I had to come halfway around the world to find you. Mitchell's *dead*. Believe me, I've seen enough dead men to know. And if you don't stop asking questions, we're all going to be joining him. I don't know about you, of course, but personally, that's something I'd prefer to avoid."

Chapter Three

Landon supposed it must have been satisfying in some way to see the shock explode in those wide blue eyes as Grace finally realized who he was. He couldn't think of any other reason for the brutal way he'd handled the revelation.

He knew he'd changed. And some of the differences were more obvious than others. That didn't excuse what he'd done, but it might help explain it.

She so obviously *hadn't* known who he was, despite the fact that he could have picked her out of any size crowd and at any distance simply by the way she carried herself. That hadn't changed, in spite of the primitive conditions she'd been living in and his suspicion that she hadn't had a real bath or a mirror since her capture.

Or maybe, he acknowledged, his response had been prompted by what he'd read in her face when he'd told her the pilot was dead. It was clear she'd been devastated, although, judging by the condition of the man in the back of the cave, she couldn't have been surprised.

He had allowed himself a few seconds to wonder

about her relationship with Mitchell before he'd forced his full attention back to the mission. Whatever—if anything—had been going on between the pilot and Grace, it was certainly over now.

His infamous luck had apparently held. It would have been hell trying to get the injured man out of the encampment and through the pass to where their transport was waiting. Thank God, Grace and Stern appeared to be in good physical condition, considering the circumstances.

"I hope you both ride," he said, his gaze still focused beyond the entrance of the cave on the sleeping camp.

Deliberately he didn't look at them. Nor had his comment been phrased as a question. He knew that Grace was an excellent horsewoman. If Stern couldn't ride, he would have to manage the best he could.

It had been impossible to get any kind of vehicle to the plateau where their captors had set up their camp. That was the intent in choosing this location, of course. If Landon couldn't figure out a way to get a truck or a Hummer up here, then neither could the Special Forces units who were searching the border for the missing Americans.

"I *have* ridden," Stern whispered, "but…I'm afraid it's been a long time."

"Like riding a bicycle." Landon had no idea if that was true, but there was no point in discouraging Stern. Not now.

He watched the silhouette of the guard assigned to the perimeter of the camp cross in front of the central fire. He was patiently waiting for him to reach the most distant point of his patrol before they made their move.

"We go to the right when we leave," he instructed in a whisper. "Keep close to the rocks and watch your footing. Make any noise, and we're all dead. The horses are in a rope enclosure about a hundred yards away."

"Won't they follow us?"

Obviously, the colonel hadn't seen enough John Wayne movies. Their captors might try, but once he freed the horses, taking them along as they rode away, any tribesmen who followed would be doing so on foot.

"We take the horses with us," Landon said, watching the steady advance of the perimeter guard.

He had already dispatched the one stationed at the entrance of the cave by the simple expedient of breaking his neck. Despite the obvious preparations the group had made for leaving the encampment, all of which he'd watched at sunset, the sentinels had been surprisingly lax.

Or maybe they were overconfident. After all, they had managed to avoid everyone who'd been sent to find them. Why should they believe that tonight would be any different?

"Now."

As he whispered the command, Landon slipped out of the entrance. In a crouching run he headed toward the corral where the movements of the grazing horses had hidden his approach tonight.

The clothing he'd bought in a village more than a hundred miles away carried in its fabric the same smells as the robes worn by the men with whom those animals were intimately familiar: sweat, smoke and dust.

He hadn't worried about Grace and the colonel betraying their presence among the horses. After three weeks of living in a cave, they, too, would undoubtedly smell the same to those sensitive noses.

Landon glanced back to track their progress. The flickering firelight, enhanced by shadows cast from the peaks surrounding the encampment, made it difficult to follow their movements. Which was exactly what he'd been counting on.

He took time to check the remaining guard, who, having reached the point most distant from camp, had taken the opportunity to smoke. Landon watched him raise the cigarette to his mouth, the tip growing brighter as he drew on it and then brought it down again.

He felt Grace ease to a stop beside him. He could hear her breathing, soft but irregular from the run she'd just made. He waited until Stern joined them, knowing it would be better if they made their raid on the horses together. Hopefully, by the time the sleeping tribesmen were aware anything was amiss, they would be mounted and away.

Hopefully.

"What about saddles?" Stern leaned across Grace to whisper.

He sounded worried, as he probably should be. Landon had anticipated from the first that the colonel could be the weak link in the escape, but after all, Stern wasn't his chief concern.

He had known Grace could easily pull this part off. She had almost made one of the Olympic equestrian teams when she'd been a teen. He had remembered that when this rescue had still been in the planning stages.

Actually, he remembered everything she'd ever told

him. That particular piece of information had been revealed in a conversation about their childhood memories. One they'd shared during a long rainy afternoon they had spent mostly in bed.

And of course conversation hadn't been all they'd shared that day. Which was something it would be better not to think about right now.

"They leave them saddled," he assured the colonel.

Most of the time that precaution made sense. It provided a means for a fast getaway, in a region that was rife with conflict. Although the soft saddles were probably like nothing either of them had ever ridden before, the fact that the horses were kept saddled was one of the things Landon had believed would make success possible when he'd come up with the idea to steal them.

He watched as the sentry's cigarette was carried upward again. Then suddenly its red tip disappeared from sight. There had been no arching glow that would indicate he'd thrown it down. Apparently the guard had turned to look out over the sheer rock face that guarded the mountainside approach to the camp.

"Now," Landon whispered, making his move toward the horses.

He didn't look back, not even when he found the rope that had been stretched across the mouth of the narrow fissure where the animals were penned. Entrapped by that and the rock walls at their backs, the animals were effectively corralled for the night and yet ready at a moment's notice.

The three of them were about to do exactly what

Grace's captors would have done if the camp had been raided. Once mounted, they would jump the low rope barrier and ride across the plateau and start down the steep, winding trail these same animals had been brought up only days ago.

As Landon moved among them, searching for the brown and white mare he'd chosen for Grace, the horses began to mill, trying to avoid the humans in their midst. He finally captured the mare, grasping her simple rope bridle to draw her with him. He turned, looking for Grace, and realized she was attempting to help Stern catch the lead of one of the others.

"Grace," he hissed.

Unable to see the guard or his cigarette because of the press of horseflesh, Landon had no idea if anyone in the camp was yet aware of what was going on. With the noise the horses were making, however, he knew it wouldn't be long before they did.

He dragged the mare over to where Grace was trying to control a big roan long enough to allow Stern to get his foot into the stirrup. The ineptness of the colonel's technique was agitating the horse, making his task even more difficult.

"Here." Landon attempted to take Grace by the elbow to direct her toward the mare. She resisted, jerking away from him almost angrily.

"What the hell's the matter with you?" he demanded. "Get on the damn horse."

"When Colonel Stern's mounted."

Landon could tell by the set of her mouth that she meant what she said. He could argue with her until the camp was aroused or he could do what he should have done in the first place.

"I'll see to Stern," he snapped.

He pressed the mare's lead into her fingers, which automatically closed around it. Then he took the roan's bridle, pulling the horse's head down firmly and holding it.

"Get up," he ordered.

The older man made a valiant effort, eventually managing after another failed attempt to pull himself into the thin saddle. By then, Landon could hear shouts coming from the direction of the camp. Apparently the guard had finally finished his cigarette and figured out something was going on.

Landon flung the roan's lead up to Stern. Without waiting to see whether the colonel would take charge of his mount, he turned to find Grace already in the saddle. In contrast to the roan's restiveness, her mare stood docilely, having already acknowledged her control.

"You'll have to ride through the center of the camp," he directed, looking up into her pale face in the darkness. "No matter what happens to me or Stern, just keep riding. There are Special Forces units all over this area looking for you."

"Aren't you coming?"

"Right behind you." As he made that assurance, he caught the stirrup of a bay that had been pushed against him by the restless herd.

"Can Stern—"

"I'll take care of Stern," he shouted, knowing by the commotion he could hear quite clearly now there was no longer any need for stealth.

"…to get separated."

In the process of swinging into the saddle, Landon hadn't caught the whole of that. It wasn't important, he decided. All that was important now—

Directing his mount near the rear of Grace's, he brought the flat of his hand down on the mare's rump. He would never have done something like that if he hadn't had complete confidence in Grace's abilities. A faith that was clearly justified.

The mare surged forward, attempting to fight her way through the throng of milling animals. She approached the low rope at a dead gallop, and with Grace's urging, easily cleared it.

Landon turned to search for Stern. He found the colonel still trying to get the roan headed in the direction of the plateau. He dug his heels into the flanks of the bay, urging him through the mass of horses, which seemed to seethe now with a life of its own. There was only one solution to the problem presented by the colonel's ineptitude in the saddle.

"Hold on," Landon yelled before he reached down and cut the rope barrier with the knife he'd taken from inside the belt he wore over his tunic.

He kicked his mount again, sending it thundering across the plateau and toward the tribesmen who were now stumbling out of tents and caves, weapons in hand. He glanced back to see the other horses following his lead, and Stern still miraculously astride the roan.

Ahead of them Grace had reached the center of the encampment. A dozen hands grabbed at her as she rode through the midst of her captors. Undeterred by their attempts to stop her, she, too, was urging her horse on, seemingly indifferent to the men who tried to slow her by throwing themselves in front of the mare.

Go on, Landon urged silently, his own mount racing across the open ground. Behind him he could hear the panicked horses pounding over the hard-packed earth of the plateau. They would provide a much-needed distraction, but he knew now there was too much distance between them and Grace.

He should have gone first. He should have left Stern to fend for himself and taken care of the woman he'd come here to find. He should have—

One of the reaching hands had locked around the mare's lightweight saddle. Although the horse was still moving at a near gallop, the tribesman showed no inclination to give up his hold. He clung on the horse's side, literally being dragged along the ground like an anchor.

And his grim determination finally paid off. He slowed Grace's mount enough that another man was able to grab the stirrup on the opposite side. Instead of being dragged, he ran alongside the flagging horse.

Grace struck at him repeatedly, using the end of the lead like a whip. He refused to let go, despite several direct blows to the face.

Of course, if they allowed their captives to get away, the consequences would undoubtedly be severe, especially for those who were supposed to be on guard tonight. Tribal justice in this setting was both swift and harsh.

By now gunfire had been added to the shouts echoing off the towering rocks that surrounding them. Landon could only hope that the Afghans, surprised from sleep, were firing wildly rather than taking aim at the riders in their midst.

He glanced behind him again, realizing only then how close the stampeding horses were. Stern was still clinging to the back of his, but it was obvious that's all he was doing. The animal was out of control, running wildly with the others.

Landon turned back toward the center of camp in time to see Grace being pulled off the mare. Although she fought desperately, she was overpowered by the three men who had surrounded her horse.

One of them grasped her from behind, his arm encircling her waist as he attempted to drag her toward the cave where Landon had found her. Once inside, and with the camp now fully aroused, Landon knew he'd never be able to get to her again.

Stretched low over the neck of the bay, he spurred the horse directly toward the man holding Grace. When he reached them, he pulled up, his mount rearing against the sudden sharp drag on the bit.

With the Glock he'd taken from his belt, he took aim, blocking from his mind the reality of how close that blond head was to the dark one of her captive. He fired just as the bay's front hooves returned to the earth.

Without waiting for the man he'd shot to fall, Landon held out his hand, controlling his mount with his knees and thighs. Without hesitation Grace put her fingers into his.

At the same time she put her left foot on top of his boot, which was still in the stirrup. He pulled, and, as if this were a trick they'd rehearsed a thousand times, she vaulted onto the back of the bay, settling behind him.

As she did, the first of the panicked herd reached them, knocking down the other men who had helped stop the mare. Once more Landon dug in his heels, his mount mingling with the horses charging through the camp, flattening everything in their path. There was another wild volley of shots, but he didn't look back, aware that because of her position behind him, Grace was exposed and highly vulnerable.

Aware also that at the other side of the plateau was that treacherous trail, part of which he'd explored last night. Steep and rugged, it was dangerous in daylight. To traverse it in the darkness, riding a horse that was on the edge of panic, would be near suicidal.

Near was the operative word, he decided, feeling Grace's arms tighten around his waist. There was no limiting adjective involved in what would happen if they turned back now.

"Hold on," he said unnecessarily, giving the bay his head as the horse began the plunge down the mountainside.

Chapter Four

By necessity Grace's fingers were locked in the coarse fabric of the long vest Landon wore over his tunic. She lowered her head, pressing her cheek against his spine as she held on for dear life.

Since Landon had shown up, a hundred emotions had bombarded her, coming at her so rapidly that she was almost overwhelmed. Right now fear was primary, of course. Concern for Colonel Stern. Rage and grief over Mitchell's senseless and tragic death.

She was also aware of a strange sense of self-betrayal. During the long days of their captivity, she had come to terms with the possibility that she would die.

After her talk with Mitchell last night, she had also reconciled herself to idea that it was too late to change anything about the way she had lived her life to this point, even if she wanted to. Although she had determined she would fight to her last breath to stay alive, she had reached a necessary inner peace about whatever fate had in store for her.

Until tonight. Until Landon James had unexpectedly

taken a hand in the game. And, she admitted, until her
body had once more come into intimate contact with the
hard, unyielding muscles of the only man she'd ever loved.

She had been aware that Landon was no longer employed by the Agency. She had also known—only because she had finally broken down and asked
Griff—that he wasn't working for the Phoenix. The latest information Griff had had was that he was operating as an independent security consultant, primarily for
companies forced to operate in the world's hot spots.

Now, surprisingly, he was back in Afghanistan, trying to engineer a rescue of her and Stern. And unless the
State Department was footing the bill, she couldn't
imagine why he would be.

"Hang on," he said again, throwing the words over
his shoulder.

As if she could do anything else, she had time to
think, before she was literally forced to obey. The bay,
which had been galloping at a breakneck speed down
the trail, suddenly veered sharply to the left, allowing
the horses behind him to sweep by on the right.

She turned her head in time to see one of them lose
its footing on the treacherous trail. Stones ricocheted
down the sheer rock face of the mountain, taking the
floundering animal with them. Its scream as it fell echoed off the cliffs and ridges.

The bay, sides heaving, was slowly being forced to
a stop. Tired, and its initial panic spent, the trembling
animal gradually obeyed the hand on its reins. Landon
guided the horse against the wall on their left at a point
where the trail widened slightly, holding the exhausted

animal there almost by force of will as the rest of the herd roared by.

Although Grace tried to peer through the darkness as the horses passed, she saw no sign of a rider on any of them. As the last stragglers came down the trail, Landon began to dismount.

Startled, she automatically tried to hold on to him, but he swung his right leg over the horse's neck and slid out of the saddle. As soon as he was on the ground, he held up his arms to her, indicating that she should dismount, as well.

Except this made no sense. They had had the advantage. They were on horseback, while their pursuers were on foot.

All they had to do to be safe was ride into the valley below. Landon himself had told her there were people looking for them there, so why in the world—

"Get down," he urged as she hesitated.

"What are you doing?"

"Trying to get you out of this mess, but I swear I'm beginning to believe you like the lifestyle. Get off the damn horse, Grace, before I pull you off."

He took a step forward, preparing to put his hands around her waist. She knew he would do what he'd threatened, no matter how much she protested. He was ruthless enough to manhandle her if he believed it was necessary.

In an attempt to keep him from touching her, she slipped her foot into the stirrup and swung down from the saddle. As soon as she hit the ground, he reached around her and slapped the bay on the rump, just as he had done earlier to her mare.

As the animal skittered nervously forward, Landon hit it again, sending it down the trail with a couple of others who were bringing up the rear of the stampede. As the horses clattered away, Grace could hear shouts coming from the direction of the camp.

A pursuit was being organized. Some of her former captors might even be mounted by now, if they'd been able to catch the stragglers from the string Landon had freed.

He grabbed her hand, pulling her along the sheer rock wall that rose high above their heads, blocking the stars. They'd gone less than twenty feet when Landon ducked, dragging her down with him.

Her first thought was that he'd heard someone behind them. Then she realized he was guiding her through the entrance of another of the natural caves that dotted these mountains.

This one, in contrast to the spacious cavern where she'd been held prisoner, was small, its entrance low and narrow. Once they'd squeezed inside it, she realized how very little room there was. Landon immediately pushed her against the stone wall and then pressed his body over hers, shushing her attempted protest.

"Listen," he hissed into her ear.

For several long heartbeats she obeyed, not daring to breathe as their pursuers came nearer and nearer. And she'd been right about the horses. At least some had been caught. Their riders shouted questions and directions to one another as they bolted past the narrow entrance that concealed their hiding place.

Despite the danger of having her captors only a few feet away, Grace was conscious of Landon's body pressed against hers. She tried to put his nearness out of her mind, thinking instead about what might have happened to Colonel Stern.

He had probably been recaptured before he could get out of the camp. After all, if it hadn't been for Landon's intervention, she, too, would have been retaken once she was surrounded.

As hard as it was for her to believe, considering the terms on which they'd parted, his principle concern had seemed to be getting *her* out rather than mounting a rescue operation that would include all of them. That wasn't enough for her, however.

"What about Stern?"

Despite the softness of her whisper, Landon's "Shh" was as clearly a command as any he'd given out on the trail. She obeyed, but only because she understood that if they were retaken, there would be no hope for the other American. If they managed to escape, they could eventually get help and come back for Stern.

After several minutes without any sound from beyond the entrance to the cave, she put her hands flat on Landon's chest and pushed. He leaned back, increasing the space between their torsos slightly, but he refused to release her, his hips still pressed intimately against hers.

"They're gone," she whispered.

"They'll be back."

"Until they are…" she suggested, increasing the pressure against his chest.

The darkness inside the cave was almost total. She couldn't see Landon's face, much less read his expression. All she knew was that he hadn't moved away as she'd asked, other than that initial lean.

"Whatever you think you're doing, it isn't welcome." Her voice rose on the last as anger overcame her fear. "I'd really appreciate it if you'd get the hell off me." She punctuated the final sentence with another shove against his chest.

"You're wearing white."

The words were so low that for a moment she wondered if she had misheard them. And then, in a rush of understanding, she knew what he feared.

The sleeveless vest Landon wore over his tunic was black. With his body over hers and his back toward the entrance of the cave, he was effectively hiding the pale silk blouse and linen slacks she wore, as well as his own lighter-colored tunic.

Now that she'd made a fool of herself again, she thought with a trace of bitterness, she should shut up and wait for him to tell her their next move. That would be the smart thing to do, but then she'd never done the smart thing where Landon James was concerned.

"Since they're gone…" she began, only to be interrupted by a noise on the trail outside.

Landon again leaned forward, putting his forehead against hers. She didn't dare protest, not with whoever was outside so close.

Suddenly she was aware of the breathtakingly familiar scent of Landon's body. Not the dusty miasma of his clothing, but the fragrance of his skin. Something she had once known as well as her own face in the mirror.

She closed her eyes as memories washed over her in

a wave of hunger so strong nothing else seemed to matter. Not the threat of the tribesmen outside. Not Stern. Not even the very good reasons for which she had destroyed what had been between them all those years ago.

"Let's go," he whispered, again increasing the space between their bodies.

She opened her eyes, surprised to find they had now adjusted to the darkness enough that she could see his face. The dark patch and the mustache distorted his features, making them alien. And exactly what she'd thought before, sinister.

"What about *them*?"

"I think that was the last."

"But… When they don't find us down below, they'll come back."

He didn't bother to respond, taking her hand instead to lead her toward the lesser blackness that represented the cave's narrow entrance. He stooped beside it for a moment, checking the trail outside. Then he slipped through, obviously expecting her to follow.

Once outside, she took a deep breath of the cool night air, letting it clear her head as her eyes examined the trail below. Landon had apparently been right. In the distance she could hear the occasional shout and the sound of horses clattering over the rocks as her captors searched for them. They had been fooled by his trick, just as he'd anticipated.

"Now what?"

He turned at her question. "We go up."

"Up?"

"Back toward the plateau."

"But…"

"Don't worry. We'll skirt the encampment. By the time they figure out that we aren't down there—" he tilted his head in the direction of the valley below "—we'll be on the other side of the mountain."

The other side of the mountain…

She looked up, her gaze tracing the peak that seemed to reach to the sky. The tribe's horses had struggled up the trail to where they'd set up camp, and that was less than a third of the way up the mountain.

Surely Landon didn't intend for them to cross it on foot and without supplies. Not even water, she realized, her heart sinking.

"Let's go," he said once more, putting his hand under her elbow to urge her up the trail.

"You're seriously proposing that we go over the mountain?" she asked as she automatically began to follow him.

"Not over the top. There's a footpath that skirts around it. It won't be easy, but…we don't have a lot of other choices."

As if to punctuate his words, from below came the sound of an explosion. It was clearly not the small-arms fire she'd heard the day the chopper had been brought down. This was ordinance, only she had no idea who could be firing it.

"What was that?"

"It sounds like an unexpected reception for our friends."

Unexpected to *him*? Or only to the tribesmen he'd sent down the trail? Had they encountered the Special

Forces operatives Landon had told her were in the area? The ones who had necessitated the expected change in location of the camp.

If so, then why were the two of them headed in the opposite direction? Why weren't they attempting to make contact with the good guys?

"Is that—whatever's happening down there—something you arranged?"

"Thanks for the vote of confidence. I wish I had that much influence."

"You said people were looking for us."

"They are. Somewhere. Maybe even down there. The problem is I don't have way of knowing who that is. And until I do, I don't intend to initiate contact. Sorry to disappoint you, Gracie, but for the time being we're on our own."

"Don't call me that."

She was already beginning to breathe more rapidly with the pace he'd set, but she thought she heard him laugh. That had always been Landon's reaction to anything that even remotely smacked of her trying to tell him what to do. He wasn't a man who took direction. Not about anything.

"Anna Grace Chancellor," he said, mocking her anger over the nickname only he had ever used for her. "So who the hell did you piss off enough to end up in Afghanistan?"

"The same people you did, I imagine."

The words were a little breathless, her voice lacking force as she struggled to keep up. It didn't matter how loud those words had been, of course. Even if they'd been whispered, they were cruel enough to carry their own impact.

Whatever had driven Landon James from the Agency had happened here in Afghanistan. That much she knew. But there had been a conspiracy of silence—at least as far as she was concerned—about the details.

He turned, looking at her over his shoulder. "You *have* changed."

"Everybody changes. It's been a long time."

"Not long enough, it seems, that you've forgotten."

Or forgiven, she thought. "Have you?"

"Only the unimportant things. This is where we go across."

He stopped, allowing her to catch up. Despite the gunfire from the valley below, in the nighttime stillness she could hear the labored sound of her own breathing.

The moonlight illuminated the path he was indicating they should take. Even in comparison to the steepness of the trail that led up to the plateau, the ascent looked impossible. It ran straight up the rock face, hand and toe holds invisible in the darkness.

"I hope all those years of sitting behind a desk haven't taken too great a toll."

Without waiting for a response to his gibe, Landon began to clamber over the rocks, seeming to locate the next hold intuitively. Grace watched him for maybe ten seconds before she admitted that, no matter how she might feel about him, she had no choice about this.

She could follow Landon, or she could wait here for her captors to find her. Mike Mitchell was dead, and Stern might be, as well. Although she had not felt the affinity for the colonel that she and the pilot had quickly found, he had been another American. Someone to talk to. Someone with whom to share her concerns about whatever was going to happen next.

If she broke with Landon, then she would be on her own. And very much alone.

It had already become evident that the tribesmen who'd captured her were unwilling to negotiate an exchange. She and the others had been held for some purpose, and without knowing exactly what that purpose was...

She put her hand on the rock, pulling herself up onto the slope Landon was climbing. She could hear him above her, but she refused to look up, fiercely concentrating instead on finding the next fingerhold.

After all, there would be plenty of time after tonight's journey was over to wonder about what would come next. And time, too, to worry about the very different kind of danger being in such close proximity to Landon James would pose for her emotions.

Chapter Five

Exhausted, Grace lay in the small shade provided by an overhanging rock. Although she hadn't moved since she'd collapsed, she hadn't closed her eyes because she was watching Landon. He lay on his stomach, looking over the top of the ridge they would now have to pick their way down.

She should probably join him. At least seem interested in the terrain that lay ahead.

Instead she closed her burning eyes, trying not to think of anything but the few minutes' reprieve she'd been given. Based on experience, she knew this rest stop would be only long enough for Landon to survey what lay ahead and plan the next leg of their journey.

When they had begun to climb last night, she had underestimated his preparation. She should have known that Landon would have thought everything out before embarking on something like this.

At the first rest stop, they had picked up the supplies he'd cached there on his way down. In addition to the long loose tunic intended to cover her Western clothing, there had been two goatskins full of water. As soon as she'd pulled the garment on, he had slung one of the skins over his shoulder and handed her the other.

Thankfully, they had been drinking from the one she carried, so that as darkness had given way to dawn and the morning wore on, the container had grown increasingly lighter. If he allowed the water break she was now eagerly anticipating, they would finish the contents of this skin and she could leave it behind.

As she thought about the blessed coolness of the water against her parched lips and throat, Landon eased away from the ledge. When he was far enough from its edge to ensure that no one watching the mountain would be able to see his movements, he straightened, walking over to where she lay.

Once there, he stooped down beside her, balancing on the balls of his feet. He examined her face, quickly coming to a decision.

"We'll stay here until the sun goes down."

The words were like a stay of execution. She would never have asked for the concession, but now that he'd made it, relief that she didn't have to immediately begin the next phase of their descent made her want to weep with joy.

She'd heard that expression all her life. Until this moment she hadn't truly understood what it meant.

"Are you sure it's safe?" As soon as the words were out of her mouth, she wanted to take them back. If he changed his mind...

"As safe as we can probably be. They don't seem to be looking for us up here."

He didn't suggest that her captors weren't still searching for them. Just that they hadn't yet figured out Landon's strategy of going in the opposite direction from the one they might have been expected to take.

"Are you all right?"

He had dragged her halfway across a mountain, pushing her relentlessly through the night and the morning with very few breaks for water or rest. The physical toll of the pace he'd set, especially after the relatively inactive weeks of her captivity, was undoubtedly reflected in her eyes and face.

"I'm *fine,*" she lied, refusing to admit her exhaustion.

She was aware that her nose and cheeks were sunburned, despite the traditional Afghan scarf that had accompanied the tunic. Now that they were apparently settled in for the afternoon, however, she realized there was no reason to continue to wear it. She removed the headpiece, running her fingers through her damp hair.

"Water?"

She looked up to see Landon holding out the horn cup attached to the goatskin she'd carried. Perversely, some part of her wanted to refuse the offering, but her cracked lips and dry throat overrode that ridiculous rebellion.

Only when she reached for the cup did she realize that her hands were still trembling from the climb they'd just made up the particularly sheer face to this ledge. As her fingers closed around the cup, one of his—long, brown and seemingly unscathed by the mountainside—traced over an abrasion on her knuckle.

She jerked her hand away, spilling a little of the precious water. The long drink she allowed herself gave her an excuse to close her eyes, so she didn't have to meet his.

When she had drunk her share—and probably more—she lowered the cup. She used the back of her hand to wipe a trace of moisture from the corner of her mouth. As she did, she looked up, catching Landon's gaze on her face.

"Finish it," he ordered.

"I've had enough." Another lie, but they always said the second was easier than the first.

For a long moment he held her eyes without taking the vessel she held out to him. Finally his lips flattened. He reached out and took the water and then, tilting his head back, he finished what the cup had held in one smooth draft.

As he swallowed, a drop of water escaped, sliding through the ebony whiskers and along the smooth, brown skin of his throat. Mesmerized, she watched until it disappeared into the high neck of the tunic he wore.

When she raised her gaze again, his was once more focused on her face. Infuriated by her inexplicable fascination with his every move, she turned her head, deliberately looking out over the vista of rocks and sky.

The sun, now at its zenith, mercilessly burned everything beneath it, including her damaged skin. She scooted farther back into the shade of the overhang, leaning against the relative coolness of the shadowed stone behind her.

Landon reattached the cup to the mouth of the goatskin. Then he laid it to the side and eased down beside her, stretching long legs out in front of him. He closed his eyes and crossed his arms over his chest, his head against the rock at their backs.

From his posture it was obvious he intended to sleep. Considering that neither of them had gotten much rest last night and that Landon planned to continue their descent as soon as the sun went down, that appeared to be a good idea.

When she tried to follow suit, however, she realized quickly how uncomfortable the position he'd assumed really was. She shifted, trying to find one more conducive to rest.

"Here." He reached out and grabbed the nearly empty water skin, pulling it closer. "Not down perhaps, but better than rock."

Down as in a pillow, she realized. And he was right. The skin would be better. There might even be enough of the tepid water left inside to make it cool, as well as soft.

"I'm fine."

"I don't remember you being a liar, Gracie. Why start now?" He tossed the skin down, leaving it to lie between them like the accusation he'd made.

"I wasn't a lot of things then that I am now."

"Like persona non grata at the Agency."

She couldn't read his tone, something that had once been second nature to her. The comment itself seemed mocking, so she responded in kind.

"I was ordered to testify before Congress. That isn't an invitation one can turn down."

"Maybe not, but *you* told the truth. How very un-CIA of you."

"Is that why they sent you for me?"

"The Agency? They haven't had the ability to send me anywhere in years."

"Then who did?"

"A mutual friend told me you were here."

"A mutual *friend*?"

"It's not as if we have that many."

"Cabot?" she guessed, now that he had thoughtfully narrowed the field. "I thought Griff no longer had the ability to send you anywhere, either."

"He doesn't."

"Then…are you saying you came here of your own accord? To find *me*?"

There had been a definite reaction to that thought. One that was distinctly physical.

"You didn't think I would?"

"I didn't think about you at all."

That wasn't true, of course. But she hadn't once imagined Landon coming to Afghanistan to look for her. Not even in the nostalgic fantasies she'd engaged in after Mike's suggestion that she should try to reconnect with the man she loved. Given his experience in this region, Landon would have been the ideal choice by either the State Department or by Cabot for such a mission, but the idea that he would agree to undertake her rescue hadn't crossed her mind.

"You always did know how to flatter a man's ego," he said with a laugh.

"I never noticed yours *needed* flattering."

She didn't know why she was determined to respond to everything he said with a display of her own bitterness. Whatever his motives in coming, Landon was here. And he had probably saved her life. Why couldn't she manage a few simple words of gratitude?

"Would it surprise you to know that I have the same vulnerabilities as everyone else?"

"Yes," she answered, mocking her own resolve.

He laughed again, this time seeming genuinely amused.

"So what are you going to do about Stern?"

Although her question was designed as a change of subject, the fate of the colonel was something that had bothered her throughout the night. She understood that they could do nothing for him as long as they themselves were in danger of being captured. Now, however, when even Landon admitted that no one was following them, they should be able to formulate some plan to find their fellow American.

"What do you *want* me to do?"

She ignored the sarcasm, plowing on with what she'd been thinking. "If they moved camp, as we believe they intended, then…we won't have any way of knowing where he is."

"The entire U.S. command is looking for him, Grace. *Whatever* they did—"

"Not here. They obviously don't know where to look."

"I gave him a horse, and I provided a distraction. I can't feel too much guilt that he didn't take advantage of it."

"Landon, we have to try—"

"What we *have* to do is to get down this mountain and across the border as quickly as possible."

"Into *Pakistan*?"

"It's safer."

"Even though it isn't under coalition control?"

"Neither, apparently, is a great deal of Afghanistan. A hell of a way to run a railroad, Gracie."

That had been one of Griff Cabot's favorite sayings. Far less graphic than its military equivalent, the catch phrase had been used by the EST for any significant screw-up, especially those made by their own government.

"Other than the border regions—" she began.

"Save the PR for someone who'll believe it. There's still plenty of real estate here available for terrorist operations. Especially in these mountains. Only the government in Kabul has changed, not the dynamics of the country. Other than the increased production of heroin, of course," he said, inclining his head in her direction.

Obviously a reference to the impossibility of her assignment. No matter how hard she tried or how innovative her approach to the problem, she would never have been able to eradicate a trade that had been going on since the Middle Ages. Even the repressive measures of the Taliban hadn't been able to shut down the pipelines completely.

Rather than argue that untenable position, she closed her mouth and turned her head, again looking out at the heat-hazed horizon. Despite the promised afternoon's rest, she wondered how much longer she would be able to keep up with Landon. Of course, if the option was to admit she was physically incapable of doing that—

When hell freezes over. An event that seemed far less likely to her right now than at any other time in her life.

Since begging for more downtime wasn't an option, she should probably make the most of the few hours he'd allowed her rather than argue about things they would never agree on. Without looking at Landon again, she pulled the goatskin he'd offered to her side of the shade. Then, still ignoring his nearness, she stretched out, using the carrier for a pillow.

And he'd been right, she realized immediately. The skin was both soft and cool. Despite the fact that the rest of her bed was still stone, she felt her tiredness and despair begin to ease in her enjoyment of the feel of the goatskin under her burning cheek.

She closed her eyes, more to relieve their dryness than with any intention of actually going to sleep. It was too hot for that. And too uncomfortable.

Besides, with Landon so close, she probably wouldn't be able to relax enough to drift off. At least she could rest, she thought, and replenish her reserves in preparation for the time when he would tell her they had to go on.

"TIME TO WAKE UP."

At the sound of that voice, Grace opened her eyes. She was looking up into the dark, lean face of the man kneeling beside her, his hand again on her shoulder.

She'd been dreaming of him, she realized. In the way of dreams, she couldn't remember what had been happening, but she remembered the feel of his lips moving over hers. Then to open her eyes and find him bending above her…

Perhaps she was still caught in the net of the

dream. For whatever reason, almost without her volition, her fingers lifted, touching the unfamiliar mustache that lined his upper lip. It was far softer than she'd expected.

The movement again unplanned, her thumb traced across his lower lip. Although it often seemed stern, almost hard, she had long ago discovered that his true nature was indicated by its fullness.

It moved now under her touch, his mouth opening slightly. For an instant she expected him to kiss her thumb as he'd done so many times in the past. He continued to watch her instead.

Other than that seemingly involuntary parting of his lips, he didn't move again until she laid her palm against his cheek, much as she had comfortingly shaped Mike Mitchell's. Landon turned his head slightly so that her fingers were no longer in contact with his face.

It was obvious he didn't want to be touched. Not by her. And just as obvious that whatever the reason he'd come to find her, it hadn't been to renew the physical relationship they'd once shared.

Although she was embarrassed by what had just happened, other than explaining that he'd awakened her in the middle of an erotic dream about *him*, she couldn't think of anything to say that would explain her actions. She began to push up instead, realizing that every muscle in her body was stiff.

Considering that climbing mountains was something she didn't do on a regular basis, that was hardly surprising. The thought of continuing what they'd done last night in this condition, however, made her want to cry.

Except she was no more willing to give Landon James that satisfaction than her captives.

"Don't you think you can discard the disguise?" She looked pointedly at the patch that covered his right eye. "There's no one up here to see you. Besides, it can't be easy judging distance with that thing on."

His lips closed, tightening into a straight line. And then he opened them to ask, his voice cold, "What disguise?"

She almost answered before she realized there was no mockery in his tone. The single dark eye held on hers, daring her to pursue the subject.

What disguise? That question made no sense unless...

She looked away, breaking the contact between them in order to deal with the revelation. Was that part of whatever had happened to him here in Afghanistan? Part of what had made him leave the CIA even before the dissolution of the External Security Team?

"Finish the rest of what's in there," he said, nodding toward the skin she'd been sleeping on.

Again, stupidly, she thought about refusing. She unscrewed the cap instead and poured the remaining water into the horn cup.

"What about you?" she asked before she raised it to her lips.

"I've had mine."

Her eyes considered the still-bulging sides of the skin slung over his shoulder. It appeared as full as it had been last night. If he was attempting to save the water for her at his own expense—

Then that must mean he knew more than he'd told her about the difficulties that lay ahead. There should be enough water for them both if all they had to do was to finish the descent.

Although she hadn't asked, she had assumed all along that Landon had arranged for some form of transportation at the foot of the mountain, just as he'd left the water skins and the clothing she wore hidden on the trail. If he hadn't, and he was expecting her to walk across the border, she would need every ounce of strength and resolve she possessed.

She tilted her head, draining the water from the cup. Then she replaced the cap and held the goatskin pouch up to him. He took it, sliding it as far back under the overhang as it would go, before he held out his hand.

After running her fingers across his mouth, like a schoolgirl with a crush, it would be silly to refuse to take his hand. Besides, the way the muscles in her legs and back ached, she was afraid she might literally need help in getting to her feet.

She reached up, putting her fingers into his. Without any visible effort, his pulled her up.

For the first time since he'd awakened her, she became conscious of the darkening sky. Landon had kept his promise. The sun that had burned relentlessly all day was sinking below the horizon. Soon the chill of the desert night would set in, and the memory of today's heat would seem like a fantasy.

Traveling in the darkness would be easier for so many reasons, not the least of which would be that she would no longer have to see whatever had been in that single dark eye when she had touched his face.

Chapter Six

"Son of a bitch."

Although Landon had muttered the expletive under his breath, on some level he had known Grace would hear it. But then there seemed little point in trying to keep this disaster from her.

The truck he'd purchased across the Pakistani border wasn't here. Nor was the man who was supposed to have driven it to this spot and then waited for them to meet him.

Ahmad was a former Afghan freedom fighter, who had once battled Russian tanks from horseback. He was also someone Landon had worked with innumerable times during the years he'd spent in this country. Someone he had trusted implicitly because he had never failed him.

Not until now.

"What's wrong?" Grace asked.

"Our transportation hasn't arrived."

He turned to look at her over his shoulder, reading exhaustion in her eyes, as well as her posture. Despite the demands he'd made, however, he hadn't once heard her complain. Not even when they'd finished the water in the second goatskin sometime before dawn.

"Are you sure this is the right place?"

Landon didn't bother to answer, knowing he was likely to take out his frustration with the situation on her. The question would have been reasonable under almost any other circumstances. When your life depended on having transportation across miles of desert, however, you didn't make that kind of mistake. You couldn't afford to.

There was no doubt in his mind about the location he and Ahmad had agreed upon. This was territory that was very familiar to them both.

"Landon?"

"I'm sure," he said, the words clipped.

"So…what do you think happened?"

That was something he'd rather not speculate on. He still believed that if Ahmad were physically capable of it, he would have been here. Since he wasn't…

"Nothing good."

That bleak assessment was honest. Although the region was a hotbed of terrorist and militia activity—on both sides of the border—arranging for Ahmad to meet them here rather than farther inside Pakistan had seemed worth the risk. Landon had had no idea about Grace's physical condition. Or that of her companions.

Maybe he'd just been hoping for some of the luck he'd become famous for through the long years of covert missions. Something he didn't seem to be getting on this one.

"What do we do now?" Grace asked.

It was a damn good question. Unfortunately he didn't have an answer for it.

With the intensity of the sun and the time that had passed since their last fluid intake, they had perhaps an hour, two at the most, before they would begin to suffer the effects of dehydration. And the water and supplies he had planned to use on this phase of their escape had been stowed in the back of the missing truck, along with his satellite phone.

He hadn't wanted to carry that into the camp of Grace's captors because if he were captured, it would have been a dead giveaway of his ties to the West. Actually, he had hoped not to have to use that form of communication at all, not with the Agency's "eyes in the sky." He had no proof the CIA had anything to do with Grace's captivity, but until he had her safely on a plane back to the States, he preferred they had no idea she was with him. Or that he was even here.

He looked up from the place where the battered Toyota should have been waiting. A seemingly endless stretch of sand and rocks lay between their current position and the nearest outpost of civilization.

It wasn't that the area was uninhabited. The problem was that it was impossible to know where the loyalties of the tribes who lived along this stretch of border might lie at any given moment. Those changed, depending on who was high bidder for their services.

Thanks to Cabot, Landon was carrying enough cash to offer some bribes of his own. In the person of Grace Chancellor, however, he was carrying something that would have a far greater value than the money.

"We go down and take a look around," he said in answer to her question. "Maybe there'll be some indication of what happened."

He didn't expect any startling revelations from the rocky ground, but maybe he could determine if Ahmad had arrived and had then been attacked. Besides, even if they were forced to continue from this point on foot, they would have to make this final descent. They had come far enough from the encampment of Grace's captors that, without water, there was no turning back.

Son of a bitch.

This time he refrained from expressing his growing anxiety aloud. As smart as Grace was, she would eventually figure out without any help from him just how much trouble they were really in.

WHEN THEY REACHED THE BOTTOM of the slope, there was no visible indication that the truck or Ahmad had ever been here. The hard-packed dirt of the road, in actuality little more than a trail, was constantly scoured by the wind, making it impossible to track the passage of a vehicle.

While he'd surveyed the area, Grace had leaned against a boulder and watched. She'd asked none of the questions he'd been expecting. Of course, she'd already voiced the relevant one. And he still didn't have an answer for it.

"Landon."

He'd been stooping, balanced on the balls of his feet, as he tried to glean any information from this desolate piece of earth. In response to an unexpected note in

Grace's voice, he raised his head to find her staring at the rocks behind him.

Even before he turned, the hair on the back of his neck began to lift. His survival instincts were well honed, but he'd had no warning this time.

His first thought was that the men who stood behind him, their Soviet-made SKS rifles pointed at his belly, must have been waiting here for whoever the truck and its driver had come to pick up. His second, a more logical one, was to wonder if that *were* the case, why they hadn't left the vehicle in place in order to lull his suspicions?

Of course, that ploy had hardly been necessary, Landon acknowledged, since he hadn't had a clue anyone else was around. Certainly not the six or seven stone-faced guerrillas confronting him.

He thought about trying for the Glock stashed in his belt. As his gaze moved along the ridge above, he was able to pick out at least a half dozen other fighters stationed behind the natural coverage the rocks provided, their weapons also pointing at him or at Grace. The odds didn't inspire confidence for any kind of fast-draw contest.

The man nearest him, taller and broader than his companions, gestured with a quick lift of the muzzle of the newer and more sophisticated AK-47 he held, urging Landon to get up. Moving carefully, he stood, at the same time bringing his hands away from his body in a universal sign of surrender.

There was no sound at all but the ever-present wind. He waited, expecting to feel the impact of a bullet in his gut at any second.

Disguised as he was, there was nothing to indicate to these tribesmen that keeping him alive might prove profitable. Grace, on the other hand…

"We need a guide to take us across the border," he said in Dari, deciding to make his proposition before they came to the inevitable conclusion that he'd be less trouble dead.

Although Dari, the Afghan version of Farsi, was one of the two principle languages of country, considering the polyglot linguistics of the border regions, Landon had no way of knowing whether they would understand a word of he'd just said. And even less reason to believe they might be interested in hiring out as guides.

Especially when they realized that a far more lucrative and less strenuous proposition was at hand. Despite the loose robe and turban that again covered her fair hair, it wouldn't take them long to recognize the potential value Grace Chancellor represented.

Of course, there was always the possibility they didn't know about the massive search for her and her fellow prisoners taking place on the other side of the mountains. If not, they would have no incentive to return her to an area where the coalition forces might stand a chance of finding her.

Even if they didn't, they would still recognize how profitable an American woman could be to them. They could sell her to the remnants of the Taliban, who had once ruled Afghanistan. Or to Al-Qaeda, who would love to get their hands on a senior CIA analyst, for propaganda purposes if nothing else. Or they might just decide to use her for their own pleasure.

Which meant Grace had probably been better off before his "rescue," he acknowledged bitterly. Apparently Cabot's faith in his abilities had been seriously misplaced.

Maybe he'd been out of this game too long. Maybe things had changed too much in a region he had once known like the back of his hand. Or maybe, he admitted with brutal honesty, he wasn't the operative he'd once been. And Grace would be the one who would pay the price for this failure.

"Who are you?"

Something nagged at Landon about the accent of the man who had gestured with his weapon for him to stand, but he couldn't put his finger on what it was. At least the leader spoke the language, which meant they would be able communicate.

Now he needed to settle on which story to try and sell them. Since they might already know some of it, sticking as closely as possible to the truth seemed the best plan.

"A friend was supposed to meet us here with transportation," he said instead of answering what he'd been asked. "He didn't show up, and now we have no way to get to Peshawar."

The dark eyes of the man with the AK-47 didn't change. Nor did the aim of his weapon, still pointed at Landon's heart.

"I have funds there," Landon went on. "I can pay you something now, and the rest when we reach Peshawar."

"You have business in Peshawar?"

"My wife and I—"

"Tell your wife to remove her scarf."

Fear cut through Landon's chest, as cold and sharp

as the blade of a knife. "Surely you don't wish to dishonor her before these men…"

He was silenced by another movement of the automatic weapon. This time it was clearly threatening.

"Do it. Do it *now* before I lose patience and blow a hole in you."

Before Landon reached the unpleasant conclusion that he had no choice but to obey, Grace reached up and pulled the scarf off her head, revealing her hair.

"Grace Chancellor, I presume?" The mocking question had been asked in English—American English— its only accent a slight Southern one. "We've been looking for you," the man with the AK-47 continued.

"Then…I suppose *I* should presume you're Special Forces," Grace said, smiling at him. "Army?"

The weapon that had been pointed at Landon's midsection didn't waver, even as the man returned her smile. In response to his expression there was a slight relaxation along the line of the dozen or so men arrayed behind the rocks at his back.

"Forgive me if I don't provide that information, Ms. Chancellor. Some of us who are presently searching for you are normally occupied in slightly more…irregular activities. I hope you'll understand." The American's eyes considered Landon's face a moment before he added, again speaking to Grace, "I should have introduced myself. Operating this far from civilization one quickly forgets its conventions. Steven Reynolds, Ms. Chancellor. Very much at your service."

The name had been followed by neither rank nor affiliation, information Reynolds clearly didn't intend to provide. He was undoubtedly one of the lone wolf operatives who worked with tribal groups sympathetic to the goals of the coalition. Although the intelligence they provided about this lawless region was invaluable, their job was incredibly dangerous.

"What can you tell us about your captors, Ms. Chancellor?"

"Very little, I'm afraid. I'm not even sure who held us. Or why. All I know is that they moved us every time the coalition forces got too close."

"And who's this?" The muzzle of Reynolds's gun was raised slightly to indicate Landon, who was still standing with his hands raised.

"A friend. He rescued me from the camp where I was being held. Somewhere on the other side of the mountain."

The black eyes assessed Landon, but there was no response to her information. And no change in the focus of the weapon.

"And your name?"

For some reason, Landon was reluctant to supply it. Maybe that was nothing more than a caution created by years of covert operations. And listening to his gut was something else he'd learned from Cabot.

"John Sloan." That was an alias he'd used on other missions.

"And you were out here looking for Ms. Chancellor on behalf of…?"

"A friend of Ms. Chancellor's in the States sent me to find her." He didn't add "since no one else seemed able to," but the implication was there.

"I see," Reynolds said, obviously picking up on the implied criticism. "You're to be congratulated, Mr. Sloan. You were able to accomplish what the rest of us couldn't. And I wonder just how you managed to pull that off." The suspicion that kept Reynolds's weapon pointed at Landon was reflected in his voice.

Since he himself would have been just as leery of someone else in this situation, Landon could only respect his caution. Reynolds knew nothing about him other than Grace's acknowledgment that he was a friend. And this was a region where friendships mattered less than anything else.

"Since I was traveling alone, I slipped in under their radar."

Reynolds nodded as if that made sense. "And you went in unarmed?"

There was no point in prevaricating. The American could always have him searched. Something he preferred to avoid.

"Hardly."

"Then perhaps you won't mind if I asked you to lay your weapons at your feet. Strictly for Ms. Chancellor's protection, you understand."

"That isn't necessary," Grace said. "He is a friend. I can assure you—"

Unsure of what she intended to tell the special operative, Landon broke in. "It's all right."

He removed the Glock from his sash, holding the grip with two fingers. His other hand still out to his side, he slowly bent, putting it on the ground in front of him.

"Kick it this way," Reynolds directed.

When he'd obeyed, Landon looked up, brows lifted in inquiry. Reynolds nodded, which he took as permission to lower his hands.

"Any idea what they intended to do with the prisoners?"

"Obviously not negotiate for their release," Landon said. "At least not with the coalition. But then that's something everyone must have realized early on."

"What about the others?"

"Mitchell was dead when I got there."

"Mitchell? That's…the pilot?"

"Mike Mitchell," Grace said. "We tried to bring Colonel Stern out with us, but in the confusion he became separated. Although our captors were planning to move their camp before we left, it may be that in searching for us, they haven't had time. I'm sure that…Mr. Sloan could guide you back there."

The hesitation before she came up with the name Landon had given the American was slight. Landon was conscious of it, but Reynolds seemed oblivious.

"I'm not sure there's much point in that," Landon warned. "If they *have* recaptured Stern, they aren't likely to remain in the same location. If they haven't…"

He shrugged, letting the sentence trail, as his eyes met the special ops agent. Without water, the colonel probably wouldn't have survived long enough to make contact with the coalition forces, not unless he got very lucky, and the American would be aware of that.

"While you were on your own, I understand that Ms. Chancellor would be your primary concern," Reynolds said. "Now that she's in our hands and we have some current intelligence as to the colonel's location, I think we should try to locate him before they have a chance to take him out of the area."

"That's exactly what I've been proposing." Grace's voice held a hint of smugness at having someone back up her request.

Reynolds's eyes again met Landon's, conveying what looked like sympathy. "I would have done the same thing in your shoes. Only now the situation has changed."

"I still believe we should convey Ms. Chancellor to Kabul or one of the regional headquarters before we look for Stern. If he's been retaken, based on his treatment during the past three weeks, he'll be safe until they decide who they want to deal with. And if he *hasn't* been recaptured, then frankly, chances are good that he's dead. I can't see putting Ms. Chancellor at risk in either case."

"Ms. Chancellor prefers to speak for herself, if you don't mind. I'm very much in favor of mounting a search for the colonel, Mr. Reynolds. Especially now that we're in such capable hands."

Landon couldn't decide if that was a slap at his handling of things or an attempt to ingratiate herself with the American. If the former, it was deserved. If they hadn't run into Reynolds and his men, this might well have become the disaster Landon had feared as soon as he realized the truck was missing.

And he couldn't force Grace to make that trek into Pakistan. Not even if Reynolds were willing to supply them.

Besides, he didn't believe the special operative would allow her to leave, not with someone he hadn't had a chance to check out. And no matter Reynolds's nationality, Landon wasn't going to entrust Grace to anyone else. Not until she was safely on a plane back to the States.

Which meant the only option was to throw in their lot with the American and his Afghan force. They would have food and water and protection from the people who had taken Grace from the downed chopper.

Even returning to Afghanistan to look for Stern wasn't an unmitigated disaster, no matter what his original plan had been. After all, if they did that, they stood a good chance of running into a larger contingent of the Special Forces who were looking for Grace and the others.

The bottom line, however, was that he no longer was in charge. Not of Grace. Not of the situation. And not being in control of his own destiny was something that had always made him uncomfortable.

Chapter Seven

The journey back to the plateau hadn't been nearly so strenuous as the one she and Landon had made away from it. Although Grace had expected they might again be on horseback, the American's troop, as small as it was, seemed well equipped.

Reynolds had directed her into an old-style military jeep, apparently the command vehicle, while Landon had been assigned to one of the two large lorries with canvas-covered truck beds in which his men rode. Demonstrating an obvious familiarity with the region, the tiny caravan had used back trails and passes that could accommodate their vehicles to return to the Afghan side. The trip took hours, of course, but far less time than it had taken for her and Landon to cross the border.

Once Reynolds had her alone in the jeep, he had peppered her with questions about Landon and the friend who'd sent him to find her. Since, bare bones or not, that story was the truth, she had confirmed it with a clear conscience—but without providing names or motivations. If the American could be tight-lipped about his affiliations, then so could Landon.

They had reached the foot of the trail leading to the plateau late in the afternoon. Despite the unrelenting heat, they climbed steadily toward their destination without encountering a soul. Nor had they found Colonel Stern's body, something she had dreaded since they'd begun the ascent.

Then, leaving several of his men to serve as a rearguard on the main trail, Reynolds led them along the same footpath she and Landon had taken up the mountain two nights ago. The party veered away from it after only a few hundred feet to climb to an observation point above the plateau. Now they were waiting as Reynolds surveyed the site below, using a pair of sophisticated night vision goggles.

"It's deserted," he said without turning.

"Then we need to go down and bury Mitchell."

Grace didn't look at Landon as she made that demand. He'd had no choice but to leave the pilot's body behind. Still, she couldn't get the photographs Mike had shown her of his family out of her mind.

He deserved a decent burial, and they deserved to know he'd had one. She also thought they would value having something of his that could be carried home to them along with that news.

"You think he's still there?" Reynolds continued to scan the terrain below through the goggles.

"I can't see any reason for them to take his body."

"Other than to sell it."

Although Landon's suggestion had been caustic, she

couldn't discount it. In this part of the world, anti-American demonstrations, especially those that included the desecration of bodies, were high impact. All the more reason, she decided, to make sure that didn't happen to Mike.

"We need to at least look for him," she insisted.

"Grace—"

"I'll take a party down and scout things out," Reynolds said, jumping in before Landon could complete his protest. "If the body's there, Ms. Chancellor, we'll take care of it."

Reynolds's quick agreement saved her from having to argue against whatever Landon came up with next. She had known he was both pragmatic and ruthless when the occasion called for it.

And maybe he was right. Maybe there wasn't any point in burying Mike's body, but it was something she intended to see done if she had to dig the grave herself.

"I'll go with you," she offered.

Before she could move, Landon caught her arm, his fingers digging into the soft flesh above her elbow. "He's been dead for three days, Grace."

"You think that matters?"

A belated realization of what that might mean in this climate mocked that unthinking response. She wasn't about to let Landon's warning make her back down, however.

"There's no point in you going down there," Reynolds said, finally lowering the goggles and turning back to them. "We'll take care of the burial. *If* the body's still there."

As much as she hated to admit it, they were right.

There was nothing she could do for Mike now. The important thing was to see that he was buried and that his family had something to remember him by.

Even that was foolish, she admitted. They had far more to remember him by than anything she might send them. It was something *she* wanted to do, maybe because there had been so little that she'd been able to do for him during the last days of his life.

"We'd moved him toward the back of the large cave because of the heat. If it's there, that's where you should find the body."

Reynolds nodded.

"And if you could bring something back for his wife…" she went on, thinking about what might have the most meaning for Mitchell's grieving widow. "Maybe his watch or his wedding ring."

Reynolds nodded again before he turned and gave a series of quick orders, using the dialect with which he communicated to his men. Most of them rose and began gathering up their weapons, obviously preparing to follow him down to the plateau.

Three of the tribesmen didn't move, apparently having been given instructions to stay with her and Landon. Grace wasn't sure whether that was to prevent them from leaving or to protect them from some outside threat.

She supposed it didn't matter. Since they'd been forced by the situation to put themselves into Reynolds's hands, he was the one making the decisions. Something she knew Landon would hate.

He watched as Reynolds led his followers back to the

footpath. As soon as they had disappeared, he glanced around to determine the position of their guards. When he turned back, his face was set.

"It's the least we can do," she said stubbornly.

"There's *nothing* we can do for Mitchell, Grace," Landon said, finally facing her. "And he'd be the first to tell you that."

She couldn't remember the last time Landon had looked at her this directly. She had known he was furious at her insistence that they try to find Stern. Now she had added to his displeasure by her determination to see Mike buried.

It wasn't that she didn't appreciate Landon's concern It was that she couldn't abandon the men who had, during the course of their captivity, become friends.

"Since he's dead, we'll never know that, will we? All I'm asking for is something of his to take home to his wife. And the right to tell her that he had a decent burial. If Reynolds is willing to do that, I don't understand why you'd object."

"Because it's just something else that will prolong your time in Afghanistan. I came here to take you home."

"Then maybe you should have chosen your accomplices more carefully."

She regretted the words as soon as they were out of her mouth. Things went wrong even on the best-planned missions.

Landon had risked his life to come here. All she seemed able to do in return was mock his efforts.

"I didn't mean that," she said softly.

There was no response to the apology. His back to

her now, Landon continued to look down on the plateau below, his shoulders stiff. She reached out, trying to take his arm to make amends, but he pulled his elbow out of her grip.

"Why don't you try to get some sleep?" he said, his voice seeming unchanged. "It's going to be a long night."

Just like the rest of them since she'd been in this godforsaken country.

I came here to take you home, Landon had said. He couldn't imagine how much she wanted him to do exactly that.

Just as soon as she'd paid the debt she owed to Mike Mitchell's memory.

ONCE MORE GRACE AWOKE to the feel of Landon's hand on her shoulder. As she looked up into his face, she experienced another unwanted flashback to a different time and place. A time when, if he had awakened her in the middle of the night, it would have been for a very different reason.

"What's wrong?"

"They're coming back."

She glanced toward the edge of the cliff that overlooked the plateau. The sun was almost up, already limning the horizon with a thread of pale yellow. Which meant that whatever had taken place below must have occupied several hours.

"Did they find him?"

"I don't know. I thought you should have a few minutes to yourself before you learn whatever Reynolds found."

She appreciated the gesture. Her brain was fogged from too little sleep over the course of the last three days. And as far as she could tell, that hadn't been helped by the effects of the short but very hard nap she'd just taken.

Now she could hear what Landon had already heard. The sound of boots clamoring over the rocky path.

She sat up, tiredly pushing her hair away from her face with the spread fingers of her right hand. "If they were there this long, they must have found his body."

Landon held out his hand. This time, without even thinking, she put her fingers into his. Although he pulled her to her feet, she could still feel the exertions of the last forty-eight hours in every stiff and aching muscle.

As they returned, Reynolds's men joined the ones who had been left on guard. One by one they sat down beside their comrades and lit the small brown cigarettes they all smoked. Finally the American came into sight at the head of the trail. Seeing that they were waiting for him, he laid his weapon on one of the boulders and walked across to where the two of them were standing.

"Did you find him?" Grace asked.

Without answering, Reynolds unbuttoned the flap of his shirt pocket. He fumbled inside before he held out the objects it had contained, hidden from sight by his fingers.

Grace stretched out her hand to receive them, palm up. Reynolds laid the wedding ring she'd asked for, along with the pilot's dog tags, on top of it. They felt cold and damp against her skin.

Because he'd washed them, she realized. After three days, that was another act of compassion.

"Thank you," she said softly.

"And this must be yours."

Grace lifted her gaze from the items he'd given her in time to see Reynolds hold out a folding knife to Landon. For a few second, the ex-CIA operative didn't reach out to take it, but he didn't deny Reynolds's assertion.

"*Must* be? Why would you say that?"

"Because it's American made, for one thing. And I doubt they'd allow Stern or Mitchell to keep one of these."

Grace was aware that something was going on beneath the surface of this seemingly innocuous exchange, but she couldn't figure out what it was. If the knife was Landon's, why didn't he take it?

"Thanks," he said finally, holding out his hand. "I didn't realize I'd lost it."

"You never know when something like that might come in handy."

Landon didn't respond to Reynolds's comment, but he took the knife and slipped it into the folds of the belt he wore over his tunic. That was the same place he'd concealed the hand gun the American had taken this morning. She wondered briefly why he hadn't realized the knife was missing when he'd been told to give up his weapons.

She supposed it didn't really matter. Not in the face of everything else that was going on.

"What about Stern?"

She wasn't sure why she'd asked that question aloud, other than to alleviate the nagging fear that had been in the back of her mind since they'd become separated. She was terrified their captors had killed the colonel in retaliation for her own successful escape.

She'd told herself that he would have the same value to them he'd had when he was first captured. They had not only kept the three of them alive for more than three weeks, they had taken pains to keep them out of the reach of the Special Forces units searching for them. So why would they take the colonel's life now?

"There was no sign of his body, if that's what you mean."

"I was hoping he might have been able to elude them, given the conditions."

"Even if he did, and if he's hiding, I doubt he'd reveal himself to someone he didn't recognize," Landon said reasonably.

Certainly not someone attired like Reynolds and his men. If Stern had managed to survive the past three days by hiding out on the mountain, he wouldn't approach a group that looked as cutthroat as this. Not unless he, too, had no other option.

"If he *is* alive, I doubt he'd be hanging out at that encampment," Reynolds said with a laugh.

Landon's eyes met hers. He was obviously thinking the same thing she was. The plateau would be the perfect hiding place. And like Reynolds, their captors would never expect Stern to return to the scene of his captivity.

"If he is still here, maybe when we ride back down the trail—" Grace began.

"I think you should probably give up any notion that Colonel Stern made it out on his own," Reynolds warned. "If he wasn't recaptured, then he's probably succumbed to heat and dehydration by now. This isn't a climate that's forgiving of those unaccustomed to it."

"Colonel Stern has been in this country for almost a year," Grace said stiffly, feeling that Reynolds's comments were a criticism.

"Sitting behind a desk in an air-conditioned office in Kabul isn't the same as being out here without food or water. You folks ready to start back? I'd like to get down to the vehicles before the sun gets too high. We're running low on supplies ourselves."

"So you plan to restock before continuing to look for Colonel Stern?" Grace asked.

"That seems like the best plan to me."

"To restock? In Kabul?" Landon asked.

"We have our own base of operations in the mountains."

"I'd like to get Ms. Chancellor back to Kabul as soon as possible," Landon said, his tone cold but polite.

"Of course. We should be there in a couple of days. I'll need to notify central command that we have Ms. Chancellor. Then, if they tell us to bring her in, that's what we'll do."

"What else would they tell you?"

"To keep looking for Stern, perhaps. I don't know who this mysterious friend is that you work for, Mr. Sloan, but…the people *I* work for expect me to follow orders. And whether you like it or not, that's exactly what I plan to do."

Chapter Eight

Like so many people who had lived in these mountains through the centuries, Reynolds and his men used a system of caves for everything from storage to sleeping quarters. It was obvious to Landon that the caves where they'd been brought three days ago were, as the American had told them, their permanent base of operations.

Grace was sitting on one of the two bunks in the area they'd been moved into yesterday. They had been afforded a modicum of privacy by a curtain hung across the opening, but they were both aware that one of the tribesmen was stationed just beyond it twenty-four hours a day.

Landon could only suppose that putting them together, something that hadn't happened the first night they'd spent here, made it easier for Reynolds, with his limited number of men, to keep a close eye on them. Or maybe the American was astute enough to realize that separating him from Grace in the current situation would have been the breaking point.

The sunburn she'd gotten the morning they'd spent

crossing the mountain had changed from pink to bronze, giving her cheeks a healthy glow. The shirt and trousers she'd washed and laid out to dry the day after they'd arrived, however, hung loosely on her slender frame.

The weight loss she'd suffered during the weeks of her captivity and the last few days on the run was made painfully obvious by the fit of the garments she'd been wearing the day of the chopper crash. He wondered what reserves of stamina she could have left in that seemingly fragile body.

"If Reynolds has notified Kabul, they don't seem too eager to send someone out to pick us up."

Landon said nothing, knowing she would have to work her own way toward the conclusion he'd reached sometime yesterday.

"Which probably means he hasn't notified anyone, doesn't it?"

"Grace—"

"And they aren't out trying to find Stern, either, are they?"

That was the excuse Reynolds had made for his departure yesterday, which had precipitated their move. Something about his attitude when he'd told them where he was going had made Landon uneasy then. Just like the incident with the knife. And a half dozen other insignificant things that had added to his growing distrust of the American.

When they'd met up with him, Reynolds had represented the lesser of two evils. Landon wasn't sure that was the case any longer.

"I don't think that's high on their list of priorities."

"What is? Finding a buyer for us?"

A buyer for Grace, perhaps. Although there was at least one person in Afghanistan who, he had no doubt, would pay handsomely to have him back in his power, hopefully Reynolds didn't have a clue about him or about his background here. Another very good reason for using the alias by which he had identified himself.

"That's always a possibility," he admitted.

"Al-Qaeda?"

There was no need to answer that. She knew as well as he did who the primary bidders would be.

If that was Reynolds's plan, Landon couldn't figure out why it had taken more than seventy-two hours to seal the deal. With as many people as there were looking for Grace Chancellor, it seemed that the American would want to get her off his hands as quickly as possible. Of course, the same thing could have been said about her original captors.

Nothing about the delay in selling Grace to one of the terrorist groups made sense. And that was the one thing Landon had come to expect after working intel in this country.

Other than the religious fanatics, the people here were basically pragmatists. If you had a product to sell, especially one vulnerable to loss or death, you got it off your hands as quickly as possible.

"If that *is* what he intends," Grace went on, "I don't understand why he hasn't separated us. Or why he allowed you to keep the knife."

"Because he knows that, as outnumbered as we are, I don't represent much of a threat to whatever he's planning."

"He doesn't know you as well as I do."

It was almost the first personal thing she'd said to him since he'd found her. And it was hard to fathom that she could still believe that after the fiasco with the truck. He didn't bother to deny that it meant something to him that she apparently *did* believe it.

"Did you really not know you'd lost it?"

"I remember cutting the rope across the corral. After that…" He shrugged.

He couldn't believe Reynolds and his men would have examined that remote area carefully enough to discover the knife lying in the darkness. Maybe it had fallen out of his belt when he'd pulled the Glock to dispatch the men surrounding Grace's horse. That had taken place in the center of the encampment. Still, given that their search must have been carried out by torch or flashlight, he was surprised they'd found the weapon at all.

"So do you have a plan to get us out of here?" Grace asked, abandoning speculation over the returned knife.

Another question that cut to the heart of their situation. Grace had always had a knack for asking those. That's what had made her such a valuable analyst. Until she'd told Congress the truth about the Agency's intelligence failures in the Middle East.

"I'm working on it."

As much of a nonanswer as he was willing to give. There was no reason to admit that it was far easier to get *into* a guarded encampment than to find a way to get the two of them out of one.

"Promise me something, Landon."

Her voice had changed. Her blue eyes were filled

with an earnestness that made him know that whatever her request was, he didn't want to hear it. Unlike her apparent relationship with Mitchell, theirs had never been about last wishes and deathbed promises. And he didn't intend for it to become that now.

He'd held her sated body in his arms through too many pleasure-filled nights to allow the thought that he might not do that again into his brain. It would only weaken him.

"Don't start that crap, Grace."

"I've been preparing to die since the day they shot down the Kiowa. But I don't want to do it in some propaganda film that's shown over and over on their television so the jackals can enjoy the spectacle."

"You *aren't* going to die. Not publicly. Not otherwise."

"Don't treat me like a child."

"Then stop acting like one. When Cabot doesn't hear from me, he'll send someone else to find you. And the damned State Department has already got half the forces in this country out looking for you."

"I hesitate to mention it, but none of them have found me."

"Unless you count Reynolds. Maybe that's what the delay is all about." He didn't believe that, of course, but if it would keep her from imagining the same images of beheadings that had haunted his sleep last night, then he was willing to lie. "Maybe it's just taking a little longer to make the arrangements to hand you over to the coalition than any of us anticipated."

"Because he doesn't have a clue about where to find people willing to come get us, right?" Her sarcasm was obvious. "Look, I'll be the optimistic little heroine you want if you'll make me one promise."

"I'm not going to promise you anything. Except that, just as I promised Griff, I'm going to get you out of this."

And if that isn't being the optimistic little hero she'd just made fun of...

"If it comes down to that—" she hesitated, her eyes holding his before she finished "—then I want you to be the one to do it."

"What the hell does that mean?"

The chill in his gut mocked his angry question. He knew exactly what she was asking him to promise.

"I thought you EST guys all knew dozen of ways to kill someone. Even *without* a weapon. And you've still got one."

"You think I'm going to slit your throat, Grace? Or break your neck with my bare hands?"

His fury with his failure to get her out of here made those questions even harsher than his earlier one. They shouldn't be having this conversation. She shouldn't be in a position where she had to think about the possibility of a public execution, which would, just as she feared, be milked for every ounce of humiliation the fanatics could derive from it. And that she *was* having to worry about that was his fault.

"If it comes down to it, I hope you will," she said calmly, refusing to react to his anger.

"Damn you," he said softly.

He took the three steps that separated them, grabbing her by the shoulders and lifting her off the bed. She flinched at the strength of his grip, but he held her against his body, looking down into her eyes. After a moment they filled with moisture.

"Don't cry," he ordered. "Don't you ever let me see you cry."

By some monumental force of will, she blinked the tears away, looking up at him defiantly.

"You're *not* going to die. Not by my hand or by anyone else's. Do you hear me, Gracie?"

"Don't call me that."

"I'll call you anything I goddam well please when you're talking this crap."

"It isn't crap to admit the possibility—"

"Shut up, Grace. Just shut the hell up."

"You admitted that you don't know—"

To stop whatever stupid admission he might have made from being thrown back into his face, he lowered his head, fitting his mouth over hers. For a long heartbeat there was no response. And then, like a flower opening to the warmth of the sun, her lips parted.

Her tongue met his, melding to it with a long familiarity that allowed her to match its movements perfectly. It was as if the years between their last kiss and this one didn't exist.

As the kiss deepened, she put her arms around his neck, her body moving into closer alignment with his. His erection was instantaneous. And full-blown.

Nothing about the way he felt had changed, he realized. Nothing except that he was now aware of the pain of losing her. A pain he'd been too stupid or too callow to admit before.

His hands, no longer needed to hold her against him,

moved down the slender back, his fingers cupping under her hips to lift them into a closer intimacy. His mouth devoured hers, her response making it obvious that she had wanted this as much as he did. And maybe for as long.

Perhaps fear or stress played some part in what was happening between them, but right now he didn't care. He wasn't going to question her motives. He was simply going to relish the feel of her body pressed against his once more.

She broke the kiss abruptly, leaning back to look up into his face. Her eyes were slightly glazed, exactly as they had always been after he made love to her.

He could see the gleam of the moisture his mouth had left on her bottom lip. He wanted to collect it by running his tongue across it. He settled instead for wiping it away with his thumb.

"This is insane," she said, her gaze moving over his face as if she'd never seen it before.

"It's the sanest thing *I've* done in a long time."

It was. Letting Grace walk away from him all those years ago had been *his* insanity. He'd known it at the time, but he'd had too much pride to beg her not to leave.

But then, that had always been his downfall. His stupid, stiff-necked pride. Especially in situations when he believed he had nothing left but that.

"This is just the result of what's happening," she said.

Maybe it was for her. But he would have reacted exactly like this to touching her again, no matter where they were or what the situation. And he had never felt this way about another woman in his life.

During the months after she'd ended their relationship, he'd been on the verge of calling and telling her exactly that dozens of times. Maybe it wouldn't have made any difference, but maybe…

He had known what she wanted. At the time, because of the nature of what he'd been doing with the EST, he couldn't give it to her.

None of Griff's team had been married. It had been an unspoken rule. The missions they undertook were too dangerous and far too covert. It would have taken a special woman to be willing to put up with both the secrecy and the long separations.

A special woman…

There was no denying that Grace Chancellor had been exactly that to him. More special than he had ever let her know. Pride again. Or maybe fear. Especially after his last mission.

"Maybe it is," he said. "But…I think you should know that nothing has changed about the way I feel."

Some emotion, quickly masked by the fall of her lashes before he'd had time to identify it, was briefly reflected in those wide blue eyes. Before he could even try to figure out what he'd seen—

"Ms. Chancellor?"

Startled, they both turned toward the sound of that voice. Steven Reynolds was holding open the curtain that provided the small privacy they had. Before Landon could react to his intrusion, Grace took a step back, freeing herself from his embrace.

"Sorry. I didn't mean to interrupt." Reynolds's tone indicated his amusement at finding them so closely intertwined.

Screw you, you bastard, Landon thought.

He didn't regret that Reynolds had seen Grace in his arms. Maybe the American needed a demonstration of what their relationship really was.

Landon's only regret was that they hadn't had a chance to finish what they'd started. At least now he knew that eventually they would. Considering the way Grace had responded to his touch, it was only a matter of time. Something he prayed they would have.

"What is it?"

At Landon's question, Reynolds pulled his eyes away from Grace's face, making his reluctance to do so obvious. He was taking pleasure in her embarrassment, Landon realized, fighting the urge to walk across and jerk the curtain out of the bastard's hand.

"I need to talk to Ms. Chancellor. In private, if you don't mind." Reynolds smiled at her as he added the last, deliberately not looking at Landon.

"Whatever you have to say to me, Mr. Sloan should hear it, too, don't you think? After all, we *are* all in this together, aren't we?"

Grace sounded perfectly composed, despite the flush of color in her cheeks. She was too proud to back down from their captor.

As the word formed in his mind, he realized that he now had no doubt that that was exactly what Reynolds was. Their captor.

"Actually," Reynolds said, "that's what I wanted to talk to you about."

"I'm afraid I don't understand." Grace shook her head slightly.

Reynolds's smile faded. He met Landon's eyes again, but he didn't answer. Instead his lips pursed before he turned back to Grace.

"Ms. Chancellor? Outside, please." Holding the curtain with one hand, he gestured with the other toward the area beyond it.

"I don't think she wants to go with you," Landon said, his voice very soft.

"I really don't want to play the heavy, but…in actuality, Ms. Chancellor doesn't have a choice. Neither do you, Sloan. I think you've figured that out by now. So, we can do this politely…"

Reynolds turned, using his free hand to motion one of the men standing behind him into the opening. The rifle the tribesman carried was quickly pointed at Landon, making the threat clear.

"Or we can do it *less* politely." Reynolds's voice was as soft as Landon's had been. "The choice is up to you."

Choice? If he were dead, they could do whatever they wanted with Grace. Even if Reynolds were about to take her away from camp, as long as Landon was alive, there was a chance he could get free and go after her.

"If it will help you to reach the right decision, Mr. Sloan, I give you my word that Ms. Chancellor will be back here with you within the hour. I really do just want to talk to her."

"It's all right, John," Grace said as she started toward the opening. "We *are* enjoying Mr. Reynolds's hospitality, after all. I don't mind having to sing for my supper."

"And I'm sure you'd do that very well, *too*," Reynolds said, smiling at her.

The emphasis on the last word had been an obvious reference to the kiss he'd interrupted. Again Landon resisted the urge to make a stand. If he did, it would be at Grace's expense. Leaving her alone in the hands of a man he didn't trust was as bad an option as letting her walk out of his sight.

"I'll be back," Grace said, glancing over her shoulder at him, a warning in her eyes. "An hour, I believe you said?"

The last was directed at Reynolds, who was smiling again. This time it didn't seem to be in amusement. And Landon found he liked the mockery of the other better than the lust he read in this one.

"No more than that, I promise you. Relax, Mr. Sloan. You really do have nothing to worry about. You'll be well guarded, I assure you."

Reynolds nodded to the tribesman with the rifle before he stepped through the open curtain with Grace. He allowed the cloth to fall, leaving the guard, his weapon still trained on Landon, inside.

Chapter Nine

Reynolds waited until they reached what appeared to be the command center of the complex before he spoke to her again. He pulled out one of the chairs around a table covered with maps and papers, indicating that she should sit down in it.

There was no point in refusing. This was his show and, for all Grace knew, it might prove to be a lengthy one.

"So the story about a friend sending Sloan here to find you was bogus." That had obviously been a comment rather than a question.

"Not at all," Grace said. "That's exactly what happened."

"And you two went from strangers to…whatever it was I just walked in on in a few days? Nice work if you can get it, I guess."

Grace had never discussed her relationship with Landon with anyone. She wasn't about to start now. Particularly not with someone she didn't trust.

For one thing, it would be too easy for Reynolds to

put two and two together and come up with their connection as the time they'd spent working together at the
CIA. And that was something Landon clearly didn't
want him to know.

"Since my relationship with John Sloan clearly
wasn't what you wanted to talk to me about when you
came to get me…" Grace let the sentence trail, her
brows raised in inquiry.

"No, it wasn't. Now that I'm aware of your attrac-
tion to the man, however—"

"Whether I'm attracted to Mr. Sloan, or to anyone
else for that matter, is really none of your business. If
you'll excuse me, Mr. Reynolds…"

She started to rise, only to have the American put his
hand on the top of her shoulder. He didn't grip it, but
the pressure he applied against her collarbone was
enough to force her back down into the chair.

"Now that I'm aware of what's going on between the
two of you," he began again, still holding her in place,
"for your own protection, I think I should warn you."

She took a breath, trying to control her temper. Not
only was he refusing to let her leave, he was also touching her without her permission. Something she hated.

She knew that her dislike of this kind of familiarity,
as well as her coloring, had gone a long way to earn her
the nickname by which many at the Agency referred to
her. The first time they'd made love, Landon had
laughed at the idea of her being called The Ice Maiden.
Since she'd ended their relationship, however, she'd
taken care to live up to that reputation, hoping that refusing to allow anyone to get close to her would prevent

her from ever again suffering the kind of pain he'd caused her. Something she'd apparently forgotten today when he'd kissed her.

"Warn me about what?" She met Reynolds's eyes as she asked her question and then looked pointedly down at his hand, still resting on her shoulder.

He removed it, his lips pursing slightly. "About Sloan."

"As I said, our relationship is none of your concern."

"Since you're in my hands right now, your well-being *is* my concern, Ms. Chancellor. And I don't intend to let anything happen to you. You're too valuable to too many people."

She laughed at his description. "You mean valuable as the person who's going to solve the heroin problem in Afghanistan, I presume. Surely you know what a joke that is."

"Valuable as someone who poses a serious risk to the image of the United States. In this region, people don't like women in positions of power. In case you hadn't noticed," he added with a smile.

"Are you saying that my position puts me in danger?"

"I'm saying that as a representative of your country, you are a very visible portrayal of what many in the area see as Western decadence. The opportunity to humiliate you—and through you, the United States—is one that some here would pay a lot of money for."

"I understand that. I've understood it since the day they brought down the chopper. I don't see what that has to do with Mr. Sloan, however."

"I'm not sure whose interests he represents."

Reynolds was worried about Landon betraying her?

Was that what the delay had been? Had he been trying to dig up information about the mythical John Sloan?

"That's not something you have to worry about," she said aloud. "The friend who sent him to find me is very real, I assure you. And his interests are the *only* ones Mr. Sloan represents."

"Are you sure about that?"

"More sure than I am about who *you* represent."

"Let's just say that you and I also have some mutual friends who are very concerned about your welfare."

Mutual friends?

"Do you mean…in the Agency?"

He laughed. "What's the old line? I could tell you, but then I'd have to kill you."

"I imagine my security clearances are higher than yours, Mr. Reynolds. Or is that even your name?"

"For the time being. But then I suspect I'm not the only one using an alias, am I? Did you ask him how he lost his knife?"

"I beg your pardon?"

Although she and Landon had discussed the knife Reynolds had found, she didn't see what possible role it could play in the conversation she and the American were having now.

"Or why he had taken it out in the first place?" Reynolds went on.

"For what it's worth, I do know the answer to that. The horses had been herded into a natural fissure in the rock face. Someone had stretched a rope across the opening to keep them in. It's a trick any horseman knows. Even if they can jump it easily, they won't."

"Except that wasn't where we found Sloan's knife."

"I'm sorry? I really don't understand where this is going."

"You sent us down there to bury Mitchell's body. Aren't you interested in how he died?"

"I *know* how he died. From a massive infection that began in the bullet wound in his thigh."

"He *might* have died from that. Eventually. Apparently someone couldn't wait for his illness to do the job, however."

"What does that mean?"

Even as Grace posed the question, a coldness settled in the bottom of her stomach. Landon was the one who'd told her Mike was dead. He said the pilot had been dead when he'd gone back to wake him.

And no one other than Landon had entered the cave after she'd said good-night to Mitchell. She would have known if they had since she'd been sleeping between the pilot's pallet and the cavern's entrance.

"Mitchell died of a stab wound to the heart," Reynolds said. "There was enough blood on the front of his shirt to make us curious, so we opened it."

"I don't believe you."

On some level, however, she did. At least she believed it was possible.

Landon knew her well enough to know that she would never leave the pilot behind. Not if he were alive.

She and Stern had both acknowledged that, given the seriousness of his condition, Mike might not survive the night. Was Landon ruthless enough to have finished off a man who was so clearly dying? A man who couldn't possibly survive the climb over the mountain that had been at the center of his plans to get them away. A man who would have gotten them all killed if they'd tried to take him with them?

She knew the answer to those questions. And she also knew that Landon would never have left Mitchell in that encampment alive. Not to bear the brunt of their captors' fury when they found her and Stern gone. Nor would he have allowed the pilot to be used for anti-American propaganda.

But if Landon believed it was the only way he could get her out of the situation, she also knew that he was capable of finishing Mitchell off without a second's thought. He might even have thought he was being merciful.

Mike would have been the first to say that was exactly what Landon should have done. Still, there was no way she could accept that sacrifice as right or moral.

Not even if all of them had died in the attempted escape?

"Whether you believe me or not is up to you, of course," Reynolds went on, speaking into her silence. "I'm just telling you what I found. And you heard Sloan. He didn't deny the knife was his."

He hadn't. Which argued *against* the scenario Reynolds had just painted.

"But if he *had* done what you accused him of, *wouldn't* he deny it? It makes no sense for him to claim ownership of a knife that would tie him to a murder."

"I doubt he considered Mitchell's death in that light. You said the pilot was dying. Besides, maybe Sloan thought the knife might come in handy sometime in the future." The subtle mockery was back in Reynolds's eyes.

"It was too great a risk," she argued, wondering which of them she was trying to convince. "It was always possible that I might have gone back to say goodbye. Mike and I—" Her voice broke unexpectedly.

"I really doubt Sloan would have allowed you to do that, Ms. Chancellor, even if you had tried."

Landon *had* prevented her from seeing the body. Forcibly prevented her.

And now it seemed there were only two reasons he would have been so determined. Either Mitchell had still been alive, only to be murdered later by their captors as an act of revenge or because they'd realized the futility of trying to take him with them when they moved their camp. Or Landon had done what Reynolds was suggesting.

Actually, there was a third possibility, she realized. Reynolds could be lying about the whole thing. To drive a wedge between her and Landon? Because of the kiss he'd just witnessed?

"How can you know it was Sloan's knife that killed Mike?"

Reynolds laughed, despite the macabre nature of her question. "I didn't have the means to do a forensic analysis, if that's what you're asking. In my time here, I've become far more familiar with wounds and the weapons that cause them than I ever wanted to be. I compared the width of the wound in Mitchell's chest to the width of the blade on that knife we found. Not conclusive, of course," he added quickly, forestalling her attempt to argue with that conclusion. "Certainly not in a court of law. But based on my experience, I'd say the match was close."

Close enough to make her doubt the man she had once loved? If she confronted Landon with this, she wondered if he would bother to deny an act that would probably have made sense to any of the three men in the cave that night.

"And you believe you could determine a match to *any* degree of certainty? Considering the number of knives that must have been in that camp."

"Are you saying you left Mitchell there alive when you and Stern made your escape?"

"Not to my knowledge."

"Then you have to consider, with both you and Stern sleeping inside the cave that night, who would have had an opportunity to put a knife into his chest."

Motive and opportunity. The two things the cops always looked for when they tried to find a killer. And Landon was the only one who seemed to have had both.

"Despite how it sounds," Reynolds went on, "I'm not trying to convince you of anything. It was obvious to me that you cared about Mitchell. I thought you should know what we found. Considering your…relationship with Sloan."

"There *is* no relationship. At least not the kind you're suggesting."

"Fair enough. Then I won't mention this again. Whatever happened, Sloan was successful in getting you away from your captors. For that, we should all be grateful. And now it seems we've had some success in locating Stern."

That news certainly wasn't what she had expected when she sat down for this interview. As she'd told Landon, she had no longer believed Reynolds was even looking.

"Where is he?"

"He was recaptured the night you escaped, by the group that held the two of you originally. They're traveling north with him, apparently trying to arrange an exchange."

"With whom?"

"With the last people on earth the State Department would want to deal with, I can assure you."

"Al-Qaeda," she said softly.

"I'm afraid so."

"So…why are you telling me?"

"Because with your help—if you'll give it—we're going to try to get Colonel Stern back safely."

IT HAD BEEN LESS THAN THE HOUR Reynolds had promised when Grace pushed aside the curtain. The man who had been standing guard over him in the meantime stepped back through the opening, his rifle trained on Landon's chest until he had disappeared behind the curtain Grace let fall back into place.

"What's wrong?"

One look at her face and he had known that whatever this was, it was something bad. That was one reason Grace could never have succeeded as an operative. Whatever she felt was revealed in her features.

"Reynolds says they've located Stern."

"And?"

"They're going to try to work out an exchange with his captors."

"Offering them what?"

Even before she answered him, Landon knew with a cold certainty what the bastard planned to do. Or at least what he had told Grace.

"He thinks they'll bite on a chance to exchange Stern for me," she said.

"Because you're worth more on the open market."

"Supposedly. If they buy into it, then he'll pretend to arrange a meeting."

"Pretend?"

"Instead of an exchange, it will be an ambush. He and his men are going to take Stern away from his captors."

"And you believe him?"

"I can't see what would be in it for him to give me to someone in exchange for Stern. As you said, I have more market value. If he's lying, then why?"

"To get you to trust him. How do we know he isn't working with whoever has Stern?"

"We don't. We don't know anything about any of them. Except that the people who held the three of us made no attempt to return us to the coalition. And now Reynolds says they've recaptured Stern and are trying to sell him to Al-Qaeda."

That, at least, made sense. If the colonel had survived, in Landon's opinion, he would have to be back in the hands of his former captives.

"Reynolds might even be on the up-and-up," she went on. "We have no way of knowing that, either."

"Did he tell you who he's working for?"

"He implied for the Agency. Something about he and I having mutual friends."

"Did you believe him?"

"Does it matter? We've run out of options, Landon. We can cooperate with Reynolds on the off chance that he is one of the good guys or…" She raised her brows. "Do *you* have another plan?"

"Where's the meeting going to be?"

"I don't know. He didn't share that kind of information. All he said was that I'm the only bargaining chip valuable enough to lure them to it."

"I don't like anything about this, Grace. Not with you as bait."

"I don't think he really cares what you like. And for what it's worth, I didn't get the impression he was asking my permission, either."

"Would you have given it?"

"To retrieve Stern? Of course."

It was only what Landon expected her to say, although he believed the connection she'd made with Mitchell, a man nearer her own age, had been stronger.

"You don't owe Stern anything. You certainly don't owe him your life."

"If Reynolds is telling the truth, it won't come to that."

"And if he isn't?"

"I don't know. All I know is that he isn't offering us a choice. We leave in the morning."

"We?"

Landon was surprised by the information. If he had been Reynolds, he would have wanted to separate Grace from Landon's influence, as well as from the possibility that he might try to throw a wrench into the scheme if he saw it wasn't what it was supposed to be.

Did that argue that they could trust Reynolds? Or did it simply indicate that he was playing a smarter game than Landon had given him credit for.

"He says his force is too small to split and still have any chance of rescuing Stern."

Which meant Reynolds didn't want to leave someone here to guard him. Landon could understand that.

The expedient thing to do in that case would be to shoot him and have done with it. The fact that Reynolds apparently wasn't proposing to do that made him wonder if he'd misjudged the man. But that wasn't something that could be decided here and now, of course.

Whatever the outcome of tomorrow's journey, it would determine one thing for sure—exactly how far they could trust Steve Reynolds. And Landon knew it would be up to him to figure that out before something bad could happen to Grace.

Chapter Ten

Even though Reynolds hadn't been able to spare anyone to keep Landon guarded back at camp, he must have decided that his plans for an ambush could succeed without the two men who were still keeping an eye on him. And obviously keeping him away from the action, as well.

They had taken Landon to a position off to one side of the ridge where Reynolds's men were hidden among the rocks, much as they'd been that first morning. Although Landon and his guards were positioned as high above the clearing as the rest of the American's force, they were several hundred feet away.

All Landon had been able to do was to watch—and worry—as the hours between midnight and dawn slowly dragged by. Reynolds's men had climbed the ridge last night, long before the proposed exchange was to take place. He'd first had his scouts search the area to make sure the people holding Stern weren't planning the same sort of double cross.

Landon shifted his position, trying to ease muscles

cramped from the long night's waiting. Then he again focused his attention on the woman sitting in the jeep below, which had been parked at the foot of the ridge where Reynolds's tribesmen were hidden. Despite the intensity of the sun, Grace had hardly moved since the American had pulled the vehicle into position almost an hour ago.

Landon looked up from the top of her fair head for a moment, his gaze following the ridgeline. From below, there would be no evidence of the ambush Reynolds planned, his troops carefully positioned among the boulders and outcroppings.

Some sound, audible in the stillness but not yet identifiable, drew his gaze back to the scene below. On the opposite side of the clearing a plume of dust had appeared that hadn't been visible only seconds before.

Reynolds had apparently spotted it, as well. He opened the door of the jeep and stepped out, unfastening the snap on the holster that held his sidearm as he walked toward the front of the vehicle.

Once there, he turned and said something to Grace. The words were too low to carry to Landon, but in response she, too, climbed out and stood beside the still-open door.

Landon glanced back, making sure he knew exactly where the two men assigned to keep him out of this were located. Rather than watching him, both were concentrating on what was happening below. At that realization a flare of hope ignited in Landon's chest.

Grace had been right. He *did* know a dozen ways to kill a man with his bare hands. All he needed was a chance to get to them before they could get off a shot. And their inattention might just give that to him.

Like Reynolds's other men, his guards were both armed with the old-fashioned Soviet-made rifles, which was a blessing and a curse. If he attacked them, Landon knew he had a better chance of survival than if he were facing an AK-47. But even if he succeeded in overpowering his guards, the weapon he would take from them would be infinitely less effective than Reynolds's.

By now he could hear the low grind of an engine straining to climb the grade of the narrow road leading up to the flat, desolate area where the American had parked the jeep. After a moment the first of the two battered, dust-covered trucks became visible. Tribesmen sat on either side of its hood, automatic weapons in their hands. The second truck, smaller and similarly guarded, followed in its wake.

An almost forgotten surge of adrenaline flooded Landon's veins. This time, however, the eagerness with which he had always greeted the start of action at the end of a long premission wait was dampened by his worry over Grace.

It didn't make any sense that Reynolds had put her in a position that made her so vulnerable. Maybe he was hoping—as Landon was, of course—that she was too valuable for anyone to want to chance her being hit by a stray bullet. Still, to have her so exposed...

The lead truck came to a halt about a hundred feet in front of the jeep. The second one pulled alongside before it, too, came to a stop. Both drivers killed their engines, leaving only the sound of the wind whipping across the clearing at the top of the plateau.

After what seemed an eternity of waiting, a man climbed out of the passenger seat of the smaller of the trucks. To indicate he was unarmed, he held his hands out to his sides, his palms toward Reynolds, as he began to close the distance between them.

Before he was halfway across, Reynolds called out in Dari, demanding to see Stern. The man stopped, looking over his shoulder as if awaiting instructions from someone in the truck he'd just exited.

When they were given, the guards sitting on the hoods of the trucks gripped their weapons more tightly. One of them moved fractionally, almost raising his semiautomatic into firing position before he thought better of it.

"We'll see the woman first," the intermediary called back in the same language.

"She's right here," Reynolds said, taking Grace's elbow to pull her forward. "Now where's Colonel Stern?"

The man carrying on the negotiations again turned to look behind him. Taking advantage of the time that would be necessary for the exchange of information the intermediary sought, Landon glanced behind him, once more checking the position of his guards. It hadn't changed. Although both of them were watching the action unfold below, neither seemed to share Landon's own sense of tension.

Nor did they appear concerned that the bargaining wasn't progressing as Reynolds had planned. Their weapons, in contrast to those of the men sitting on the trucks, were still held loosely in their hands as they craned to see around the rocks they were supposed to be hidden behind.

Maybe they didn't understand the language, Landon thought. Still, if they knew their comrades' attack on the men in the trucks was imminent—

Suddenly the nagging anxiety he'd felt from the first exploded in Landon's gut. Reynolds's men weren't prepared for action. Not of any kind. While the tribesmen who had purportedly come to trade Stern for Grace—

His gaze quickly returned to the clearing below. The intermediary for whoever was sitting inside the second truck was only now turning back to relay his message to Reynolds, who was still holding Grace's arm.

Landon's every instinct, sharpened by years of covert operations, screamed that something was very wrong about what was taking place. He just wasn't sure who was double-crossing whom.

And at this point it really didn't matter. All that mattered was the woman who was about to be caught in the middle of it all.

"He says you are to come with us," the intermediary called to Reynolds. "We'll take you to see the American colonel."

"That wasn't the deal," Reynolds yelled back. "You were supposed to bring him here."

"He is unwell. Unable to make the journey."

"Then the deal's off."

Reynolds said something to Grace, releasing her arm and at the same time appearing to give her a small shove in the direction of the open passenger side door. She had already turned, taking a step in that direction, when the first bullet ricocheted off the jeep beside her, whining away into the blazing heat.

It was the signal Landon had been waiting for. And dreading.

Despite his growing uneasiness with what was happening, with Grace in the line of fire, he would never have dared to make the first shot. Now that someone had—and had drawn no answering fire—his suspicions solidified.

He whirled, in his hand the fist-size rock he'd selected hours ago. Ignoring his guards' attempts to bring their weapons up, he charged across the few feet that separated them, striking the one who appeared to be slightly closer to getting his rifle into firing position with a vicious upward swing to the jaw.

With his other hand, Landon grabbed the man's weapon as he toppled over backward. He brought the gun around, swinging the butt at the other guard's head, as the man finally got his gun up.

The force of the blow jarred his victim enough that the shot went wide. Shifting his hands slightly on the barrel of the weapon he held, Landon swung it like a club, bringing the stock down on the unprotected side of the man's neck. He, too, crumpled like a fallen tree.

Slinging the strap of the rifle over his shoulder, Landon clambered over the boulder the two of them had been stationed behind and then continued to climb. Driven by fear and adrenaline, miraculously he seemed to anticipate finger and toeholds in the sheer rock face that allowed him to scale it until he reached a position that would put him above the rest of Reynolds's men on the other ridge.

As he had made his move, he'd been aware he would be highly vulnerable during this ascent, both from the tribesmen below, as well as from the American's men. Bullets began to chip stone only inches from his body as he climbed, but not nearly as many as he had expected.

As soon as he reached an outcropping that would provide cover, he ducked behind it. He peered over the rim as shots continued to splinter shards from the rocks around him.

The jeep was still parked in the same spot. He couldn't see Grace, but Reynolds had taken shelter behind the vehicle and was returning the fire coming from the trucks with a hand gun.

Although bullets from the automatic weapons raked the front of the jeep, from which steam now rose, Landon held to the thought that Grace could survive even that barrage if she'd made it back inside the automobile. Especially if she were on the floorboard, placing the engine block between her and the gunmen.

Refusing to think about anything other than stopping the shots aimed at the jeep, Landon sighted through the scope and took out one of the two men on the smaller truck with his first shot. Seeing his comrade fall, the second scrambled off the hood, only to be cut down before he'd taken more than a couple of steps.

Landon then turned his attention to the occupants of the larger truck, picking off the guard on the left before he'd had time to realize what was happening. The remaining tribesman finally stopped firing at the jeep and lifted his weapon to take aim at the new threat. Landon shot him in the chest before he had time to pull the trigger.

By that time Reynolds had also turned and was looking up. He didn't raise his weapon in Landon's direction, however, so Landon ignored him, sending a round through the windshield of the truck where the person issuing the orders was seated. With the angle of the sun off the splintered glass, it was impossible to tell if he'd hit anyone, but at least the vehicle didn't move.

Before he had pulled the trigger, he had fleetingly considered that Stern might also be inside that truck. Almost as soon as the thought formed, he rejected it. If this "exchange" had been legitimate, the colonel's captors wouldn't have gone through the song and dance of demand and counterdemand. Just as his gut had told him, this had been a setup from the beginning.

The driver of the second truck had apparently gotten the message that someone was deviating from the script. He started the engine and then stomped down on the accelerator, sending the rear wheels spinning through the loose dirt.

For an instant Landon thought he intended to drive the truck straight into the parked jeep. A sense of helplessness fueling his rage, he pumped a couple of bullets into its windshield, as well. By the time they made impact, it had become obvious that the driver had simply been circling to get by the other truck.

He roared around it, wheels spewing gravel, and headed down the grade over which his vehicle had strained only minutes before. When Landon's gaze returned to the smaller truck, he saw that a man was pulling the dead driver out of the front seat and dumping him on the ground. Then he scrambled in over the body, slamming the door and immediately starting the engine.

With the muzzle of his rifle pointed at the windshield, Landon waited until the replacement driver had made the same circle in the center of the plateau, following the dust generated by the first truck back down the slope. When it disappeared, he lowered the rifle he held until the crosshairs on its scope were aligned with the center of Steven Reynolds's forehead.

"Throw your gun into the passenger seat," he ordered.

There was only the slightest hesitation before the American held his hand out to the side, tossing the hand gun he'd been using into the seat Grace had occupied.

"Now call off your men," Landon said, shifting the muzzle slightly toward the ridge before he aligned it once more with Reynolds's head. "Do it now."

Whatever else Reynolds was, he wasn't stupid. "Throw your weapons down," he yelled to his men.

There was no way Reynolds could know for sure whether Landon spoke enough of their dialect to understand that command, but apparently he wasn't taking any chances.

In the resulting stillness, Landon heard the distinctive clatter of weapons being discarded onto rock. Whether all of Reynolds's men had obeyed that order was open to question, of course. That would depend on the kind of discipline the American had instilled in his force. Something Landon wouldn't find out until he put it to the test.

"Grace?" he called.

He literally held his breath until her head and shoulders slowly appeared in the narrow space between the jeep's front seat and its dash. She had done exactly what he'd hoped she would, taking shelter in the one place that would offer her some protection.

Of course, no one had ever questioned Grace Chancellor's intelligence. As she picked up the gun he'd made Reynolds pitch into the passenger seat, Landon knew he would never have cause to doubt her courage, either.

"You hurt?"

In the couple of seconds he'd allowed himself to take his eyes off Reynolds to glance over at her, he had noticed the spreading splotch of red on the sleeve of her silk shirt. She gripped the gun in her right hand, however, pointing it at Reynolds. At his question, her left crossed over her chest, touching the opposite arm just above the elbow.

"Only a scratch." Her voice sounded remarkably steady, considering.

"Think you can drive?"

There was a slight hesitation, which Landon hoped was attributable to surprise rather than any indecision about her ability. It wasn't strictly necessary, of course, but he'd feel better if he were the one holding the gun on the American.

"Of course."

"We need the trucks," he said, turning his attention back to the American. "Have someone bring them around."

Reynolds's mouth twisted in anger. "You won't make it out of here on your own. Just because something went wrong today—"

To shut him up, Landon put a bullet into the mirror on the driver's side of the ruined jeep. It struck close enough to where the American was standing that Reynolds visibly flinched.

"Nothing went wrong," Landon said. "This was a farce from the beginning. I'm just not sure for whose benefit it was carried out."

"I don't know what you're talking about. If you think—"

"Send somebody to get the other vehicles. And do it now." Landon sighted down the barrel again, but he didn't have to pull the trigger this time to provoke a reaction.

"Hakim, you and Husain go get the trucks and bring them here."

Somewhere on the ridge to his right, Landon sensed movement. Again, whether the tribesmen were acting in accordance with the verbal instructions Reynolds had given was beyond his ability to verify. He would know if those orders had been carried out only when the vehicles appeared below.

Reynolds tried again. "I don't know what you think is going on—"

"I think this was an ambush, all right, but *those* people weren't the intended victims."

"If you're implying—"

"I'm not *implying* anything. I'm telling you what I know. Nobody in the Agency wants to hand Ms. Chancellor over to Al-Qaeda. The PR damage from that would be a disaster, and they know it. And they don't want her to emerge from this ordeal to become a hero to the media back home."

"Look—" Reynolds began again, only to be ignored as Landon continued to speak over his attempted protest.

"What they'd *really* like is for her to be killed over here. Neatly and cleanly killed. *With* an appropriate witness. Someone who can verify to the authorities that her death took place, of course."

It had taken him too long to figure this out, but being that witness had obviously been his role today. There was no other reason for Reynolds to have brought him along. He was supposed to return to Washington and tell Griff Cabot about Grace's unfortunate death during a bungled prisoner exchange.

"I'll admit that something went wrong, but—" Reynolds tried again.

"The only thing that went *wrong* is Grace survived. Whoever that was in those trucks, they weren't her original captors. And they obviously didn't have Stern. Chalk this one up to a missed opportunity, Reynolds. Apparently the company *still* doesn't have the right people in place over here."

That last remark was too revealing. At this point, however, Landon didn't really care.

All he cared about now was getting Grace out of this guy's control. He hadn't completely trusted Reynolds from the beginning. Now that he knew what the man's agenda was—as well as who was paying him—he was more determined than ever to strike out on their own.

"You'll never get out of here alive." Reynolds's tone had changed, becoming less conciliatory.

"Not if we stay with you."

Landon could now hear the sound of the other vehicles being brought forward. He had known that wherever they'd been hidden, it wouldn't be too far away. After all, since Reynolds's ambush was bogus, he didn't really have to worry about his supposed victims stumbling across them.

"What are you going to do?"

"Not a thing until your men transfer the extra gasoline from the back of the larger truck into the other one. When that's done, *you're* going to order them to leave their weapons lying where they are and all get into the larger truck. And then you're going to order them to drive away."

"What about me?"

"You wait here with Ms. Chancellor and me until they're gone."

"And then what?"

The bravado in Reynolds's voice had slipped slightly with each question. Without his men to back him up, the American was simply another foreigner in a land that was particularly inhospitable.

"That depends on how well and how quickly they carry out your orders. And by the way," Landon said, switching into the dialect spoken by Reynolds's men. Although he was not even as fluent in the tribesmen's language as Reynolds was in Dari, it was enough to prove his point. "I don't think it's in your best interest to tell them to do anything except what I've told you to. I'll be listening very carefully. And the first time I don't like what I hear, then you won't have to worry anymore about explaining to the Agency exactly what went wrong today."

Chapter Eleven

"How do you know they'll go back for him?"

With Grace's question, Landon glanced over at her, taking the opportunity to evaluate her condition. Although she had assured him the wound in her arm was only a scratch, he didn't like the chalklike paleness of her cheeks.

Before he addressed her concern about Reynolds, he also looked at the makeshift bandage he'd applied. Reassuringly, there was no seepage of blood through the folds of the cloth tied just above her elbow.

"What do you care?" His gaze had returned to the track they were following.

"Because you left him in the same situation we would have been in if he hadn't found us."

"They'll come back for him eventually."

"How can you be so sure of that? Maybe they don't like him. Maybe they're glad to get rid of him."

"Except their weapons are there. Those are too valuable not to go back for. And if they don't, then there'll be one less bastard trying to wrench some advantage from this country."

"I thought you were convinced Reynolds is backed by the Agency."

"You think that means he can't be a bastard?"

"No. The CIA certainly has its share of those. But I *do* think it would mean he isn't here for his *own* advantage."

"Actually, I think he's probably an independent contractor," Landon said.

"Hired to do the Agency's dirty work?"

"In this case."

"Do you *really* think the someone at the CIA is trying to kill me? Because I testified before Congress?" Her dismissal of the possibility was clear in the tone of her questions.

"I think somebody in Washington decided this was too good an opportunity not to take advantage of."

"Meaning?"

"When your chopper went down, it was an answer to more than a few prayers."

Surprisingly, Grace laughed. "I won't argue that there weren't people at Langley who celebrated. I just can't see why they'd go to the trouble of getting someone to kill me. My testimony's a done deal. There's nothing they can do to change it."

The expletive with which Landon expressed his derision was blunt, as well as colorful. Or maybe Grace really believed that, he realized. If so, she hadn't seen the dirty underside of the Agency that the members of the EST had been exposed to.

"How can they change what's now a matter of public record?" she demanded, reacting to his ridicule. "A *very* public record."

"The reason your testimony carried so much weight was because of who you are. A highly respected, *female* intelligence analyst with a spotless record. One who had, moreover, made it to the top echelon of a very engrained, old-boy-dominated organization."

"Thank you." Amusement once more colored her voice.

"So maybe they can't change what you *said,* but they *can* change the public's perception of the person who said it. And that kind of revisionism is always easier if the person being deconstructed is no longer around to protest."

"'Deconstructed'?"

"In your case, I don't know what they'll come up with to accomplish that. Maybe that most of the intel failures you cited can be traced back to you."

"Considering the extent of those failures, I think that's going to be a hard case to make. I didn't have the power to influence policy."

"Then maybe you advised the people who did."

"Except those people are already gone."

They were, Landon acknowledged. Long before Grace gave her testimony, those at the top of the Agency deemed responsible for its failures had been forced to resign.

"Then maybe they'll claim you had a personal vendetta against one of them. Or that you were taking bribes. Even that you were working for the other side."

"Nobody who matters would believe *any* of that," she said. "It's all crap, and you know it. So would ninety-five percent of the people at the CIA. And those who didn't…"

"Maybe you're right," he conceded when she hesitated over the characterization of the rest. "But those ploys have been used at one time or another to discredit people."

"By the CIA?"

"By *some* government agency or another. They all operate on the same principle, Gracie. It's called 'cover your ass.'"

"Is it also called murder?"

"You tell *me* where that first shot was aimed today. If you hadn't already taken a step away from the jeep, that bullet would have struck the back of your head instead."

He didn't look at her, but he was aware of the depth of the breath she took. As brutal as this truth was, it was something she needed to understand. Until she grasped the reality of her situation, she was vulnerable to another trick like Reynolds's promise to help her find Stern.

As far as Landon was concerned, that wasn't a priority. The colonel was on his own. Stern was a career soldier, someone who had been in this country for several months. A chance to escape was all he felt he owed the man, and he'd given him that.

Landon had come to Afghanistan to find and rescue Grace Chancellor. He didn't think Griff or Dalton had been under any illusions about that, and they were the only people to whom he owed an explanation.

"Wherever that bullet was aimed, even if it was at me, that doesn't mean Reynolds planned it," Grace said.

"No, but the fact that his men didn't react by returning fire *does*. At least, it goes a long way toward proving it to me."

"Which wouldn't be too hard, would it? You didn't like him from the first."

"This isn't about liking or disliking. I didn't trust him. Today he justified my distrust."

"I think you're blaming him for something that was beyond his control."

"It was his meeting. His arrangements. His responsibility. And he blew it."

"So what *do* we do about Stern?"

He knew he hadn't convinced her, but apparently she had decided that arguing with him about Reynolds wasn't going to get her anywhere. So they were back to what seemed to him her near obsession with rescuing her fellow prisoner.

"It was obvious those clowns didn't have him."

"I know. I understand that. But...*someone* does."

Or—and far more likely in my opinion—he's dead.

Landon knew there was no point in saying that, either. Since he couldn't prove it, Grace was unlikely to accept it. Or accept that, even if Stern *were* still alive, they didn't owe him a thing.

"Maybe without you around, whoever's holding him will put him into the hands of the coalition."

"Without *me* around?"

"The *only* explanation that makes sense for the fact that the guys who brought down the chopper hadn't tried to negotiate for your release is that someone doesn't want you returned to the States. Apparently, they've made that clear to the interested parties."

"Or maybe my captors were trying for better terms. You can't know that they weren't dealing with...someone."

She had expected to end up in the hands of a terrorist group. If not Al-Qaeda, then one with close ties to them. Maybe even one of the groups operating on the other side of the border.

Based on the promise she'd demanded of him, that seemed to be her greatest fear. And he understood that was not because she was afraid to die, but because she didn't want the public spectacle of her death to be used against her country.

He could sympathize with her feelings. He would have expected no less from her. That didn't explain why no attempt had been made by her captors to sell her to *someone.*

"In this part of the world," he said, "you make use of the bird in the hand before it can fly away. Especially when so many people are looking for that particular bird."

And especially when life here—any life—is so damned fragile.

"So…is that where we're going? To find the people you keep saying are looking for me?"

"Just as fast as we can," he promised.

The trek across the mountains into Pakistan was no longer an option. Too many people were aware that Grace was traveling with him. And like the cliché he'd just beaten to death, far too many of them would like nothing better than to take her away from him.

"And when we find them…? Exactly how will you know you can trust *them?*"

Another question he didn't have an answer for. When he'd started this, that part had seemed simple. He would find Grace and smuggle her across the border. Once in

Pakistan, he had believed he could get her onto a plane for Washington before anyone was the wiser.

Now, given the fact that they'd literally had to fight their way out of what could only be considered a second captivity, he couldn't be sure that the "powers that be" on both sides weren't aware of what was going on out here. If they were, then they would all be looking for him and for Grace. The good guys—and the bad.

"The same way I've always figured out who to trust. Gut instinct."

She laughed again. "Now that's a logical response. Is that how Griff's vaunted External Security Team operated?"

"Sometimes." He knew that she was mocking him, but what he'd said was the truth. "Griff was always a believer in trusting his operatives. I don't know one of us who hasn't acted strictly on instinct during the course of some mission."

"That's why I would have made a terrible field agent. My instincts about people haven't proven to be all that reliable."

He glanced at her again. She had placed her hand over the makeshift bandage on her arm. Although he knew she must be aware he was looking at her, her eyes were determinedly focused on the road ahead, her lips tight.

Was she talking about their relationship? If so, he couldn't blame her.

After all, seven years ago he had given her every indication that he loved her. Because he had.

At that point in his life, however, loving someone—even someone like Grace—hadn't been enough to make him give up the work he was doing for Griff. And he'd known that's what she wanted.

A house in the suburbs. Maryland. Or Virginia. Commuting into Langley together so they could sit behind a couple of desks all day.

There had been nothing appealing to him about any of that. Nothing except Gracie.

There still was nothing in that scenario that particularly appealed to him. Like it or not, however, it wasn't far from what his life was like today. Except it didn't include the woman who, as he'd acknowledged all those years ago, might have made it bearable.

He'd made a conscious choice then, and it hadn't been what Grace had wanted. Now that what he *had* chosen had been taken away, it didn't seem fair that he'd get a second chance with her. Not even if she'd been prepared to offer him one. And so far there had been no indication she was.

"If you're talking about what happened between us—"

She turned, looking at him with what seemed to be genuine amusement in her eyes. "What in the world would make you think that?"

He studied her face before he pulled his gaze back to the road. "We have to talk about it eventually."

"I can't imagine why. It's over and done, Landon. I promise you that."

He nodded, surprised to discover how much her casual dismissal bothered him. As if he were the only one who felt regret over the way they'd left things.

In any case this was something else he didn't intend

to beat to death. Maybe she really was no longer interested. Seven years was a long time to carry a torch for someone.

And I should know…

"We need to stop and take care of that," he said, tilting his head toward her injured arm. It seemed time to change the subject from one that was uncomfortable to both of them.

"I *would* like to try to get it clean. After watching what happened to Mike—"

She stopped suddenly, drawing his gaze to her again. Her lips had closed over the pilot's name. She turned to look at him, something in her eyes he couldn't quite read before she turned her head to look out through the windshield.

Maybe she was worried that the same thing that had killed Mitchell, a wound gone septic, might happen to her. Although the situations weren't the same, after what she'd been through, he couldn't blame her for that concern.

"I have to ask you something," she said, her tone entirely different from the almost caustic one she'd used when discussing their previous relationship. "And I want you to tell me the absolute truth, Landon. This isn't the time for lies. Not between us."

"The truth about what?"

"Something Reynolds told me."

"About me?"

She nodded. "And Mitchell's death."

"I don't understand."

"He said Mike didn't die of the infection. I know it

would have killed him eventually, but…he said you did that because you knew you couldn't get him out of there alive."

"He told you I killed Mitchell?"

"When they went down there, they found bloodstains on his shirt. It didn't fit with what I'd told him. So…they opened it. Someone had stabbed him in the heart."

"And you think *I* did that."

"I think that if you thought that was the only way to get me to leave him there… And since it was obvious he was dying anyway. I think maybe…you would have."

He didn't answer immediately, dealing with the fact that she believed him capable of that. And then dealing with the question of whether he was or not.

Maybe at one time he would have been, but now… Still, Mitchell was clearly going to die that night, even if they had managed to get him out of the encampment. Would it have been better for him to have died in agony while they dragged him across the mountain, perhaps slowing them down enough that her captors caught up with them? Besides, wasn't the swift, clean death Reynolds had described to her the same merciful ending she had begged for herself.

"You wouldn't let me go back and see him," she said into his silence. "And no one else came into the cave that night. Not after I said good-night to him."

It was obvious she'd been thinking about this for a while. Adding up evidence of his guilt without giving him a chance to explain.

"Landon?"

"You asked me for the truth. I'm trying to decide exactly what that would be."

"How can you 'decide' what the truth is?"

"Mitchell was dead when I went to the back of the cave. I swear that to you on—" He stopped abruptly, his lips flattening before he opened them again. "On the only thing I hold sacred. Mitchell died of his infected wound, Gracie. Nothing else."

"If that's true," she began again, "then why would you have to think about it?"

"That's exactly what happened that night. But that isn't the only thing you asked me."

She had suggested that perhaps he'd realized the only way to get Mike out of that situation was to kill him. In other words, what would he have done if Mitchell *hadn't* been dead when he'd gone to the back of the cave?

"And if he had been alive?"

"I don't know. I came here to get you out. That's why Griff approached me. Because he believed I'd do whatever it took to accomplish that. Would I have ended Mitchell's life quickly and painlessly rather than put him through hours of unnecessary agony to achieve the same result? I honestly don't know. But I do know, from the little you've told me about him, what Mitchell would have wanted me to do if he'd been given that choice. Thank God, he wasn't. He was dead when I found him, Grace. And that *is* the truth, whether you believe it or not."

"I believe you."

He couldn't tell from her tone whether she really she did. At least she was giving lip service to trusting him that far.

"Good. Because that's what happened. And as for the other… There's a first-aid kit in the back." He'd noticed it back there on the way to the rendezvous. "There's probably some antibiotic salve, maybe even some tablets. You think the bullet's still in your arm or did it go through?"

He hadn't had an opportunity to examine the wound. He'd stopped to tie the scarf around it as soon as they'd gotten a few miles from where they'd left Reynolds. All he really knew was that Grace had called the injury minor and that it hadn't seemed to bleed very much.

Maybe that wasn't a good thing, however. He remembered reading somewhere that a strong blood flow could carry fragments of cloth and debris out of a wound.

"It's just a gash from a splinter of metal off the jeep. If there *is* salve in the kit, that should take care of it."

Landon glanced in the rearview mirror, which reflected the long empty road behind them. He had no idea where they were, only that they were traveling east, the direction in which he knew they needed to be headed.

If it would make Grace feel better, there didn't seem to be any good reason not to stop and clean the wound. When he'd done that as well as he could, he'd put a proper dressing on it.

It wouldn't take ten minutes all told, and at the same time he could add another can of gasoline to the truck's tank. Then they'd be on their way again, both of them with a little more peace of mind.

There was not a lot of shelter from the sun here— only endless miles of the same barren terrain. Which wasn't likely to change any time soon, he admitted. He allowed the truck to begin to slow.

"What are you doing?" Grace asked.

"I'm going to stop and take a look at your arm."

"It's fine. At least until we get somewhere—"

She stopped suddenly, seeming to realize, as he just had, that in the vast uncharted emptiness of this wilderness, this was as much "somewhere" as they were going to find.

Chapter Twelve

Landon didn't even bother to pull the truck off the road. He shut off the engine and then got out to retrieve the first-aid kit.

When he started to jump down from the bed, he realized that Grace had also gotten out and walked around to the back of the vehicle. She'd already begun to unwrap the strip of cloth he'd placed around her arm.

Landon laid down the metal box containing the first-aid kit, marked with its distinctive red cross. Then, using one hand on the tailgate for balance, he jumped down. Grace looked up as he landed beside her, her fingers hesitating in the act of removing the bandage.

"You want me to do that?" he asked.

"I can manage."

As she returned to the task, he slipped the knife Reynolds had returned to him from his belt. When he snapped open the blade, however, her eyes immediately came up. Widened, they focused on the knife before they lifted to his.

"I'm just going to slit your sleeve."

"But these are the only clothes I have."

It was such a totally feminine thing to say that he almost laughed. Without asking permission, he reached out and put the palm of his left hand under the injured arm. Then he inserted the point of the knife into the opening of the placket where her cuff buttoned.

He took a breath and then began to apply pressure against the opening in the sleeve. The razor-sharp edge of the blade split the silk effortlessly. He moved it upward until he reached the place where blood had glued the shirt to the wound.

He glanced up, trying to gauge Grace's reaction, but her face was averted. Afraid he might hurt her in attempting to split that section of the sleeve, he laid the knife on the tailgate.

Without looking at her again, he lifted the edge of the cloth that was plastered to her skin and began to pull it away. Although he didn't jerk the fabric up in one motion, once he'd started applying pressure to it, he didn't stop.

He heard a sharp inhalation as he peeled the last of the material from the wound. Ignoring the sound, he gripped the sleeve he'd just freed with both hands, continuing to tear along it the split he'd begun with the knife all the way to the shoulder seam.

Then he put his hand under her arm again, acutely conscious of the smoothness of her bare skin against the callused flesh of his palm. Ignoring the sensation, he turned her elbow so that for the first time he could see the full extent of the injury.

Her description had grossly minimized the damage. Long and irregular, the gash was far deeper than he'd anticipated. And it had begun to bleed anew as soon as he'd ripped the shirt away.

"What do you think?"

He looked up to find that she was trying to see the now-exposed cut, although the angle she was looking at it from was awkward.

"I think it needs stitches." Her eyes came up quickly in response to that. "And a good doctor to put them in."

"I thought you were about to claim that as another of your skills. I'd always heard Cabot's team was self-sufficient."

"That didn't extend to doing our own surgery."

"Frankly, I find that a relief."

Her tone seemed almost normal. Which was a good thing, considering that trying to get the gash on her arm clean and relatively sterile wasn't going to be pleasant. Not for either of them.

"Without stitches, this will leave a scar," he warned.

"If it does, no one will ever see it."

He wasn't sure if that was a challenge or a promise. Or maybe neither.

He hadn't wanted to consider the possibility that Grace had had other lovers in the years they'd been apart. He knew how ridiculous it was to believe she hadn't. Especially ridiculous, since he, maybe more than anyone else, knew how sensual she was.

"I'm going to wash this out first. And I should warn you before I start…"

"What?"

"I need to make sure there are no bits of fabric or

fragments of the metal still inside. I'm afraid that process is going to be—"

"Painful," she finished before he could.

"Feel free to scream," he suggested, deliberately lightening his voice. "There's nobody to hear you."

"Sorry. I wouldn't give you the satisfaction."

"Why the hell would you think I'd get satisfaction from hurting you?"

She laughed, the sound abrupt. Without any trace of amusement. "Let's just get this over with, okay? We can debate your sadistic tendencies another time."

He refused to rise to the bait. "There's some bottled water in there," he said, jerking his head toward the bed of the truck. "It's probably safer to use than what we've been drinking."

"That's not very comforting."

Without responding, he freed her arm. Before he climbed up into the truck, he automatically scanned the area surrounding it once more.

There was still no traffic on the road. And no sound but the ever-present wind.

It felt as if the two of them were the only people on the planet. As if time had ground to a halt, giving them another chance to do what they should have done seven years ago. A chance he might have been willing to take had Grace not made it so obvious she wasn't interested.

He jumped onto the truck bed again. Because of the low canvas ceiling, he was forced to crouch as he made his way to the front where he'd seen the opened carton of water. He grabbed two of the plastic bottles, taking a final look around for anything else that might be useful in cleansing the wound.

He had already turned to head back to the tailgate when he realized that, although he could see Grace, he would be hidden in the shadows at the back of the cab. He couldn't resist the opportunity to study her while she was unaware of it.

She was holding the cloth over the reopened gash in an attempt to stanch the flow of blood, but she had turned to look back in the direction from which they'd come. Tendrils of her hair, caught by the desert wind, blew across her cheek. She bent her head, using her shoulder to brush them away from her face.

As she did, she turned, looking into the back of the lorry. Her eyes, surrounded by the newly tanned skin, appeared more blue, clearer somehow, than they'd ever been before. Although he was sure she couldn't see him crouching in the darkness, the fact that he was watching her made him feel like a voyeur.

"Did you find it?"

He started forward, a bottle of water in each hand. "I was looking around for something to use as a scrub."

"Like…a cloth, you mean?"

"Yeah, but there's nothing clean enough in here," he said as he reached the tailgate.

Unthinkingly, he held out the bottles of water to her. She shook her head, lifting the injured arm slightly to indicate she couldn't take it. He put them down, once more jumping to the ground.

"Other than this…" she began, holding up the cloth he'd originally tied over the wound.

It was the remains of the scarf he'd bought for her in that Pakistani village. While usable as a tourniquet, it could hardly be considered sterile. Nothing either of them had on would meet that qualification. The closest thing—

"What about your shirt?"

She had washed out her clothing a couple of times while they'd been cooped up at Reynolds's headquarters, wearing the garments he'd supplied for their trek across the mountain while the others dried. Although the silk blouse was dusty, it was cleaner than anything else.

"There should be gauze in the kit," she suggested.

If they were lucky. But he'd planned to use that to fashion a dressing. Before he argued the point, however, it would probably be smart to see how much of it there was.

He pulled the metal box toward him, opened the rusted snap and then raised the lid. The contents looked old enough to have been left over from World War II.

There were a few gauze pads, thankfully still enclosed in cellophane packets. Under them was a bottle of Mercurochrome. As he rummaged through the remaining items, he discovered a half-empty tube of what might be the antibiotic salve he'd been expecting, but its label was so worn it was unreadable.

There were no pills. No suturing needle or thread. No roll of gauze. No tape.

Still, it was better than nothing. Unless whatever was in the tube turned out to be something other than what he was hoping it was.

"There's gauze."

He hadn't realized Grace was looking over his shoulder. He turned, finding her eyes on his face.

"Not much."

"Enough," she said. "You *make* it be enough. I'm *not* taking off my shirt."

He had once known the contours of her body as well as he knew his own. Had kissed every millimeter of her silken skin. Had tasted it.

He'd made love to her in every way he could conceive of. There had been no part of her that he hadn't been intimately—delightfully—familiar with. And now…

Her eyes changed as something of what he was thinking must have been reflected in his expression. He said nothing, simply looking down into her face. While he watched, a tinge of color spread under the bronze of her cheeks.

"Whatever you say, Gracie."

He forced his lips into a smile he hoped would appear to mock her reluctance to undress in front of him. Then he twisted the top off one of the bottles of water, setting the cap down on the tailgate.

He poured the water over one of his hands and then the other. Although he was doing little more than rinsing off the surface dirt, it was better than nothing.

When he'd finished, he picked up one of the cellophane packets and ripped it open with his teeth. He pulled out the gauze, careful to touch only one corner, and laid it out on the paper he'd removed it from before he picked up the bottle of water he'd used to wash his hands.

Grace had stepped back, putting more distance between them. When he was facing her again, he could tell by the rise and fall of her breasts, visible under the thin silk blouse, that her breathing had increased.

A dread of the procedure he'd described? Or was she a victim of the same unwanted memories he'd just experienced.

"Ready?"

"Whenever you are."

She lifted the bandage away from the wound, which was still seeping blood. Her eyes, when she raised them to his, reflected none of the nervousness he might have expected to find there.

Steeling himself, he took her arm again, gripping it more tightly than he had before. He held it up so that he had a good view of the injury, and then he poured a stream of water over the gash.

As he'd anticipated, the clotted blood was affected very little by the liquid. The new bleeding, however, seemed to increase as the water flowed over the wound.

"Use the gauze," she said.

There really was no other option. Not if he wanted to even make an attempt to clean out the injury.

He released her arm, reaching for the pad he'd already laid out. He soaked it with the water before he set the bottle down on the tailgate. When he turned back, she was holding her arm out for him.

"Do whatever you have to, Landon. And don't worry about how much it hurts. I saw what happened to Mike."

Obviously she was still haunted by the pilot's unnecessary death, but that sounded as if she believed him about its cause.

"Even if I don't get this perfectly clean, we'll make contact with our guys before anything can go wrong."

"Famous last words," she said, glancing up at him through her lashes.

He was relieved to see a teasing glint in her eyes. "Trust me, Gracie."

She laughed at that mocking reassurance. Before the sound had faded, he began to dab at dried blood on the edges of the gash.

There had been another sharp intake of breath, quickly controlled. He didn't look up, continuing to work steadily until he'd removed most of the old blood.

He tossed the gauze back on the cellophane and picked up the water bottle again. Holding the cut open by applying pressure with his forefinger and thumb positioned on either side of it, he allowed new blood to run out for a few seconds. Then he poured a steady stream of water directly into the gaping wound.

As he did, he again looked up to gauge her reaction. Her head was turned, but he could see that her teeth were set in her bottom lip.

"You okay?"

She nodded without speaking. Unwilling to waste any of the precious water, he looked back down, allowing the stream to flush the gash once more.

When he'd used the last of it, he tossed the empty into the bed of the truck. Then once more he put his hand under her arm, holding it up to the bright sunlight. He couldn't see any of the debris he'd feared might contaminate the wound, but he knew that was no guarantee it wasn't there.

"I'm going to wipe it with a clean piece of gauze," he said. "That's probably going to be less pleasant than the water."

"Got it," she said, her voice slightly muffled.

"Want me to give you a minute?"

"I want you to get this over with. Despite my crack about your sadistic tendencies, I'd really appreciate that very much."

He ripped open another of the cellophane packets, wetting the pad it contained with water from the second bottle. "Here we go."

"Thanks for the play-by-play, Landon, but...just do it. Okay?"

Again he spread the gash open, this time rubbing the gauze along its length. Beneath his fingers he could feel a slight vibration that seemed to run throughout her entire body. He didn't let it deter him, however, knowing that if he was going to put her through this, then he'd damn well better do it right.

When he finished, he poured the rest of the water over the injury, which was now bleeding profusely. Which was a good thing, he told himself.

And exactly who are you trying to convince?

Mercurochrome or the nameless salve? At least the first was a known element. He held the mangled tube up to the light, trying to read the label.

Having no more success than before, he opened the cap and squeezed a thin thread of it out on his finger, being careful not to let the tip touch his own skin.

The stuff could be anything, he decided. And as old as the rest of the supplies appeared to be, even if this had once been some kind of antibiotic, he couldn't believe it would still be potent. Besides, he had no way to tell if the last person to use the tube had been as careful about keeping the applicator clean as he'd been.

There was really no other option, he decided, putting down the tube and picking up the small brown bottle. He couldn't remember from his own childhood whether it had been Mercurochrome that had stung so badly or iodine. His mom had been a firm believer in one or the other. Not that it mattered at this point.

"This is going to sting," he announced before he remembered Grace's reaction the last time he'd tried to warn her.

Without waiting for a response, he gripped her arm again, widening the gash once more before he poured the red liquid over it. This time, with another gasp followed by a word he'd never heard her use before, Grace tried to pull her arm free. He'd been expecting it, holding on tightly until he'd emptied the contents of the bottle.

"What the hell was that?" Her mouth was slightly open, and she was breathing through it.

"Mercurochrome."

"You're kidding. I didn't think they made that anymore."

"They probably don't."

He tossed the bottle back into the metal box. Then he opened the last two packages of gauze, laying the first over the raw wound. He folded the second, to make it thicker, before he put it on top.

"You still have that strip of the scarf?"

She turned, holding the cloth out to him in her free hand. "All done?"

"Other than tying this in place."

"So what do you think?"

"I didn't see anything to be concerned about," he said, hoping that was the case. "I think it should be okay. When we make contact with the Special Forces, we'll get the medic to look at it."

"You're pretty proud of yourself, aren't you?"

"What does that mean?"

Another gibe about him enjoying her pain? If so, he'd taken about enough of that kind of crap.

"That you managed to get this clean with nothing but that." She nodded toward the rusted first-aid box.

"In addition to being self-sufficient, we were also resourceful. And accustomed to working with what's at hand."

"Thank you."

"You would have done the same for me."

"You bet your sweet ass I would. And I would have enjoyed it just as much."

It was so obviously a promise of payback that he couldn't even be angered by it. After all, what he'd done to her had hurt like hell, and he knew it. She deserved to get in her licks, even if they were only verbal.

"I'll remember that."

He began to gather up the things he'd used, deciding that he might as well put the trash back into the metal box. There was nothing left in there that would be of any use to anyone in the future.

As he looked around for the second of the empty

water bottles, a flash from the ridge on the far side of the road caught his eye. Despite the lifting of hair on the back of his neck, he continued the motion he'd begun, grabbing the bottle and sticking it into the box.

Then, as unobtrusively as possible, he pretended to look for anything else that should be stowed away while his gaze searched the rocks where the flash had originated.

After a few seconds his vigilance was rewarded. The glimmer came again from the area where he'd seen it before. He made a show of closing the lid of the metal box, snapping the latch and then sliding it toward the back of the truck while he considered what he'd just seen.

He couldn't think of anything that occurred naturally out here that would produce that effect. It would have to be something that reflected sunlight. Something like the lens of a pair of binoculars. Or the scope on a rifle.

Chapter Thirteen

"Get back in the truck," Landon said, as he shoved the first-aid kit farther back into its bed.

Grace turned to look at him, still holding the elbow of her injured arm. She couldn't imagine why his tone was so brusque. Granted, her suggestion that she would enjoy causing him pain at some future date might be interpreted as bitchy, but Landon had seemed to take it in the spirit in which it was meant.

"Get *in* the damn truck, Grace." This time he had turned to look at her, his expression grim.

"Why?"

"Because somebody's watching us from the ridge to the south."

She automatically glanced in the direction he'd indicated, but the rocky slope appeared deserted. "How can you possibly know that?"

Without answering, Landon began walking toward the front of the truck. He had already opened the door on the driver's side and was climbing into the cab by the time she reached the opposite one.

"I saw the sun reflecting off a lens up in those rocks," he said, looking at her through the open window on her side.

A lens? For a second or two she couldn't think what that might mean. "Like…binoculars?"

Or a scope, she realized belatedly. Despite being one-handed, she managed to get her door open. Although Landon was already turning the key in the ignition, she hesitated, unsure how she was going to be able to climb into the high cab. She couldn't imagine trying to use her still-throbbing arm to haul herself up.

"Here," Landon said.

She reached out and grasped the hand he held out to her. With the help of her foot planted on the running board, Landon was able to pull her up as if she weighed nothing.

She settled into the seat, putting her hand back under the elbow of her injured arm in an attempt to cradle it. As Landon shifted into drive, he examined the ridge where he'd noticed the reflection.

Whatever he believed that to be, he didn't floor the accelerator, as she'd expected from his sense of urgency. Instead, he steadily got the truck up to the speed he'd maintained before they stopped and kept it there.

"You think it could be Reynolds's men?" she asked.

"Wrong direction."

It was, of course. Landon had deliberately driven off in the opposite direction to the one they'd taken.

"Then who?"

"Almost anyone," Landon said, his gaze shifting from the road to touch again on the low ridge they were traveling parallel to.

"But… It could be someone attached to the Special Forces. Someone looking for us."

"It *could* be," he acknowledged, although he didn't slow the vehicle. "There's no way to know that *or* anything else. And it makes me very nervous to have someone watching me when *I* can't see *them*."

She didn't remember that the road had been this rough. Every bump and pothole now seemed magnified because of the sensitivity of the newly abraded wound.

"But…you can't just *assume* it's someone who intends to do us harm."

"You bet your sweet ass I can," he said, deliberately echoing the phrase she'd used only minutes before. "That's *exactly* what I'm going to assume. At least until I have a good reason to think differently."

"Then how in the world do you think we're ever going to—"

Her words were abruptly cut off as the truck topped a rise. Below them a convergence of vehicles blocked the road. In addition to a couple of lorries, comparable in size to the one they were driving, there were perhaps half a dozen pickups, most of them the ubiquitous Toyotas that were the favorite mode of transportation for the region.

A couple had been parked so that they were facing in the direction their truck was headed. Men with rocket launchers had been stationed in the beds of each of those. And right now, they looked as if they were preparing to fire.

"Christ." Landon said the word so softly it seemed an invocation rather than a profanity.

Obviously not *the good guys,* she thought.

He spun the wheel, putting the truck into a tight circle that didn't take it far off the road. As soon as the front end was headed away from the roadblock, he floored the accelerator, sending the vehicle roaring back toward the top of the slope.

Before they could reach it, an explosion rocked the truck's frame. The rocket hit near enough that gravel and a spray of dirt struck the windshield with a frightening velocity.

Unthinkingly, Grace threw up her arm, trying to protect her eyes from the debris coming in through the open window. The resulting agony quickly reminded her of why she'd been holding it so tightly against her body.

"Hold on," Landon warned.

She tried to obey, but not only was there no seat belt, there was nothing else to hold on to. She put her palm against the front of the dash, but it didn't help.

Giving up, she crossed her arms over her stomach, hunching her shoulders and sliding as far down in the seat as she could. Still, she was thrown from side to side as the truck bounced along the narrow road.

Through the partially obscured windshield, she could see well enough to realize they were approaching the place where Landon had noticed the reflection. Considering the known danger pursuing them, she supposed that unknown watcher was the least of their worries.

She could hear the now-familiar sound of automatic weapons fire behind them. Despite the noise of the straining engine, she also heard bullets ping against the metal at the back of the truck.

"Son of a *bitch*."

She turned and, through the window on his side of the truck, saw what Landon had reacted to. Horsemen streamed across the area between the southern ridge and the road. And those riders would intersect it before they could get by.

An ambush that had been far better planned than the one Reynolds had devised. Which argued Landon had been right about that, too. The ridges on either side of the road cut off any chance of escape they might have had by going across country. And with the trucks behind them carrying rocket launchers—

A bullet struck the windshield and thudded into the seat between them. The hole it left in the glass centered a spider web of cracks. As they drew nearer the horsemen, other shots began to ricochet off the body of the truck, whining away into the heated air.

"Get down," Landon ordered grimly.

As she tried to obey, she felt the truck begin to slow. He couldn't be stopping. Despite the odds against them, anything would be preferable to just giving up.

"What are you doing?"

"Trying to keep you alive. Trying to keep *both* of us alive."

"Don't do this," she begged, but the deceleration of the truck didn't change.

Landon put his left hand out the window, holding it up, elbow bent, to signify his surrender. She couldn't believe he was giving up this easily. They could have attempted to outrun the riders. They could have attempted *something*.

She'd told him the only thing she feared. And it wasn't death. At least not this kind. The quick brutality of being struck by a bullet or even of having the truck hit by a rocket would be a blessing compared to one of the gruesome executions the world had watched in stunned horror.

"We can outrun them," she argued. "They're on horseback, for God's sake."

"We can't outrun rockets. Look behind you."

Her glance through the back window revealed what Landon had already been aware of. The pickups that carried the launchers had topped the rise and were being positioned to fire again.

Far better than an execution, she thought, even as she watched in fascinated horror as the men prepared to send up the next rocket. Better, too, than the slow, lingering dying Mike Mitchell had suffered.

Except maybe he hadn't. If Reynolds was right, the man at her side had been ruthless enough—or perhaps merciful enough—to free him from his suffering. And that was all she had asked of him for herself.

"Promise me," she said, gripping Landon's arm.

"What?"

"What I asked you before."

"I *promised* I'd keep you alive. That's what I'm trying to do."

He turned to shout something out the window at the riders who were now circling the slowing truck. Apparently, whatever he said had the desired effect. The gunfire had stopped.

In the sudden, almost eerie silence, she could hear

only the thud of horses' hooves and the keening cele-
bration of the tribesmen who had forced the truck to a
halt. In response to something one of the horsemen
shouted through his open window, Landon began to
apply the brakes. As soon as the vehicle lurched to a
stop, he shut off its engine, removed the keys and tossed
them out the window.

Maybe Landon could convince them that the coalition would be willing to pay a great deal of money—

In the midst of that hopeful fantasy, the driver's side
door was jerked open. Hands raised, Landon turned in his
seat, preparing to jump down. Before he could, the horseman who had wrenched open the door reached in and
grabbed a fistful of his tunic, pulling him out of the cab.

The rider held on to Landon's clothing as he backed
his horse. Then he released him abruptly, causing Landon to stumble a few steps.

Another of the circling riders kicked at him, catching him in the back and sending him staggering forward.
Despite the blow, Landon somehow managed not to fall.

That obviously hadn't been the intent of the exercise.
Before he'd completely regained his balance from the
kick in the back, one of the riders urged his horse forward at a gallop, literally ramming his mount into him.

This time Landon went down. As he did, he covered
his head with his arms and rolled in an attempt to escape the hooves of the horse that was now being ridden
over him.

Grace couldn't tell if he'd been successful, but somehow he managed to get to his knees. His hands were
again out to his side, but Grace was unsure if that was

a sign of surrender or if he was preparing to protect himself from the next assault, which happened almost instantaneously.

Another of the riders sent his mount careering toward the downed man. Landon tried to scramble to his feet, but as the horseman passed him, he kicked out with his booted foot, catching Landon under the jaw.

His head snapped back with the force of the blow. And this time when he hit the ground, he didn't move. A couple of the horsemen circled him, apparently hoping for some further sign of resistance.

Unable to sit and watch whatever came next, Grace opened the door of the truck, sliding down from the high cab. She hit the ground too hard, falling back against the side of the vinyl seat and jarring her arm.

Ignoring the pain, she ran around the front of the vehicle, dodging the milling horses. One of the riders reached for her, catching her shoulder, but she jerked away.

She pushed past the man who had kicked Landon. Still in the saddle, he was hovering over him as if he couldn't wait to strike the next blow.

"Stop," she said in Pashto.

Most Afghans, except for those in the most isolated regions along the country's borders, spoke the language—at least well enough to understand that rudimentary command.

The man who'd kicked Landon leaned down and grabbed a fistful of her hair, pulling hard enough as he straightened in the saddle to make her eyes water. She thought that he literally intended to drag her by her hair behind his horse. Laughing, he turned to say something to one of the others.

Definitely not Pashto.

Acting on instinct alone, she reached up and, using the hand of her uninjured arm, jerked the captive strands from his fingers. As soon as she was free, she knelt beside Landon.

Her heart in her throat, she focused on his chest and was rewarded by its regular rise and fall of his chest. *Alive*. Thank God he was alive.

She had no time for more than that thought. The man from whose hold she'd just escaped jumped down from his horse, landing almost on top of her. She dodged away from him, but his fingers again tangled in her hair, using it to turn her head so that she was looking up at him.

His other hand was already raised to strike when one of the Toyotas that had been part of the first prong of the ambush screeched to a halt beside the truck. Several of the horsemen surrounding it had had to scatter to avoid being run down.

Like everyone else in the group, her assailant froze, his hand poised in midair. As the dust the pickup had stirred up began to settle, the door on the passenger side opened. In the almost breathless stillness, Grace could hear her own breathing, quickened from fear and the run she'd made to get to Landon.

The man who stepped out of the Toyota was imposing. Perhaps six foot four or five, he probably weighed well over three hundred pounds.

In contrast to the tribesmen around her, who smelled of dirt, grease and horses, he was fastidiously—almost femininely—dressed. His sleeveless weskit was snow white, and it was worn over what appeared to be a gray silk tunic, which had been heavily beaded and embroidered. His beard was precisely trimmed and gleamed with oil. On his head he wore a silk turban, arranged in a style she'd never seen before.

"Ms. Chancellor, I believe."

The flawless English, with its slight British accent, was almost more startling than his appearance. Because of that, it took a split second longer for the fact that he knew who she was to register. Despite what his men had done to Landon, there was a flutter of hope in her chest.

"Who are you?"

The fat man smiled. "I think in this situation asking the questions is *my* prerogative."

"Are these your men?"

"Acting under my orders, I assure you."

"Then your orders are responsible for their attack on a man who was attempting to surrender."

"So you say. If I asked them, I might receive an entirely different explanation."

As he spoke, he began to walk to where she was still kneeling on the ground. The tribesman had already released his hold on her hair. He began to back away respectfully as the fat man approached.

He stopped only a foot or two away, so that she was forced to look up at him. The position not only emphasized his height, but was clearly designed to place her in a subservient position.

"May I help you up, my dear?"

A ruby the size of a robin's egg gleamed on one of

the manicured fingers of the hand he held out. The entire performance was like something out of *The Arabian Nights*. As if he were some ancient pasha, offering a favor to a servant girl.

Grace didn't want to take his hand, although her own was filthy in comparison. To hide her reluctance to touch him, she glanced down at Landon, hoping for some sign that he was regaining consciousness.

His lips were parted, just as they had been when she'd reached him. The eye that wasn't hidden by the patch was closed, black lashes lying unmoving against the dark cheek.

There was nothing to indicate he was aware of what was happening. Or that he would be of any help in dealing with the man standing over her.

"Ms. Chancellor?"

His tone was still polite. When she looked up into the fat man's eyes, however, she knew that whoever he was, he was her enemy. They were as black as a piece of obsidian. And as cold.

Her options were extremely limited. Ignore the outstretched hand and struggle to her feet on her on, perhaps alienating him even further. Or put her fingers into the pale ones he had offered, at least giving the appearance of cooperation.

The flood of adrenaline that had sent her rushing fearlessly through enemy horsemen had faded to be replaced by a sense of helplessness. Although she recognized that what she was feeling had been compounded by blood loss and fatigue, the wave of despair that washed over her was impossible to deny.

Reaching up with her good hand, she put her fingers into those of the fat man. They were softer than her own and slightly moist. Her immediate reaction was one of repugnance, but the thick fingers closed around hers with a surprising strength, easily pulling her to her feet.

He released her hand immediately and turned to give an order to one of the tribesmen, who had begun to edge closer. Whatever dialect the fat man spoke, it wasn't any of the languages she had knowledge of.

"I'm afraid you'll have to ride in the back of the truck, Ms. Chancellor. It's rather crowded up front."

She could imagine it would be. And she had no desire to be crushed between his perfumed body and that of the driver.

"Come, my dear," the fat man urged. "We really don't have all day. In these troubled times, this road isn't as isolated as one might wish."

More isolated than *she* wished, she thought bitterly. Despite all Landon's talk about the people who were looking for her, they'd encountered no one from the coalition.

"What about—"

She stopped, remembering Landon's reluctance to identify himself to Reynolds. Her hesitation over his name didn't seem to matter, however, since she had turned to look down at the unconscious man.

"Ah, yes. Mr. James. I haven't forgotten him, I promise you."

Moving incredibly fast for a man of his bulk, the fat man took a couple of delicate running steps forward.

Then he drew back his foot, incased in a gleaming calf-skin boot, and kicked Landon in the ribs. The thud of the blow was audible over her gasp of reaction.

Despite the fact that Landon didn't open his eyes, there had been a definite reaction to its force. A low sound—almost a sigh—escaped the parted lips.

"Stop it," Grace said, grabbing the man's arm in an attempt to pull him away.

Again his response was both swift and brutal. He gripped the wrist of her bandaged arm, twisting it behind her back. She screamed once in agony and then sank her teeth into her bottom lip, determined to keep from crying out again as he pulled the arm higher.

Using his hold to propel her forward, he shoved her toward the back of the truck and the tribesman waiting there to help her in. Then he released her so suddenly that she stumbled and would have fallen had the tribesman not reached out to steady her.

"As I said, delay is dangerous. Especially dangerous for Mr. James. Why don't you do your friend a favor and get into the truck as I suggested. Of course, if you wish to *prolong* his suffering, I can't tell you how happy I shall be to oblige."

As if to suit words to action, he turned and started back toward Landon. Horrified, but now convinced that he meant what he'd said, Grace desperately looked up into the weathered face of the tribesman standing beside her. She thought she detected a glimmer of sympathy in the dark eyes.

He laid the weapon he carried down on the tailgate and vaulted up into the bed of the truck. Then he reached down, grasping her good arm just above the elbow. This time there was no hesitation on her part.

She put her foot on what appeared to be a trailer hitch. Then, using the last reserves of her strength, she gripped the wiry arm with her own fingers. Despite the pain, she put her other hand on the tailgate, using it to boost herself up as he pulled her effortlessly into the truck.

When he picked up his rifle, he used it to gesture her toward the front. Holding her hand under the elbow of her aching arm, she eased down on one of the ammo boxes stacked inside.

When she looked up again, two of the tribesmen were lifting Landon's seemingly lifeless body up onto the tailgate. The guard who'd helped her in bent, and with the assistance of the others, dragged it to the center of the bed.

The two men who'd carried Landon jumped down, closing the tailgate behind them. The man with the rifle sat down on another of the boxes. He leaned back against the side of the truck, his gun across his lap, his hands still positioned so that he could raise it in an instant.

In a matter of seconds she heard the engine start. Surrounded by the horsemen and a thick cloud of dust, the cavalcade began to move. Fighting tears of despair, Grace looked down at Landon, whose head lolled helplessly from side to side as the truck raced over the same rough ground they'd covered only minutes before.

Chapter Fourteen

The women who had helped her bathe had been kind, exclaiming with concern over the bandage on her arm. They had also shooed the guard with the automatic weapon—which, she noted, was neither old nor Soviet made—out of the room before they stripped off her clothes and helped her into the bath.

Although she had still had no contact with either the man who'd brought her here or with Landon, it was amazing what being clean and having something that wasn't filthy to put on had done to banish her sense of hopelessness. If their captor wanted Landon dead, she had told herself, then he could have managed that easily during their capture. The fact that he'd taken the trouble to load him into the truck to bring him to this village high in the mountains argued that Landon was still alive.

Please, God.

She took a breath, refusing to allow any other possibility into her head. Their captor knew who she was, which meant he must also be aware that the Special

Forces in this region were searching for her. No matter who he was or how powerful he believed himself to be, the might of the United States wasn't something anyone could afford to ignore.

She hadn't been able to come up with an explanation for him also knowing who Landon was. Despite thinking about all this for most of last night and today, she still wasn't sure of the implications of that. She *was* sure, however, that they weren't good. Nor for either of them.

The attack on Landon had been highly personal, she acknowledged, picking another bit of roast lamb out of the stew the women had brought her. That kick in the ribs had been delivered with a viciousness that connoted something more than casual brutality.

As she again pictured that moment, she remembered their captor's treatment of her. The hand that had been in the act of carrying food to her mouth fell. No matter how she tried to spin this, there was no getting away from the reality that they were in the hands of a sadistic bastard who apparently had a personal score to settle with Landon. And now he had the opportunity to do exactly that.

She knew Landon had spent years in Afghanistan. His last assignment before the dissolution of the External Security Team had been in this very area.

Despite her clearances, she'd never been able to learn what had happened during that mission. Obviously Griff Cabot had believed that, whatever it was, it was no one's business but his and Landon's.

Personal. Just like the fat man's attack on Landon. Which might mean…

That the man was an old enemy? She had certainly glimpsed enmity in his eyes, but at the time she'd been willing to assign that to the same anti-Americanism that drove the terrorists.

And it was possible that that was all it was. Yes, he had kicked Landon and deliberately twisted her injured arm, but then, why would she not expect that kind of treatment from the same people who crashed planes full of innocent people into occupied buildings?

Al-Qaeda.

She had known from the moment the chopper went down that they would undoubtedly be the high bidder for her and the others. And the only thing they would enjoy more than having a high-ranking CIA analyst under their control would be to have both an analyst *and* a longtime Agency operative. Two victims for the price of one. And in the end, they hadn't even had to pay for that privilege.

Or had they? Steve Reynolds was likely to be the source of the information that had allowed the fat man to set up his ambush. If Landon was right, then maybe Reynolds, having lost the opportunity to carry out his own carefully arranged execution, had decided to do the next best thing and sell their whereabouts to the terrorists.

Except, Landon also believed that Reynolds was an independent contractor working for the Agency and that having her end up in the hands of Al-Qaeda was the last thing the CIA wanted. It would be very bad for their image, both at home and abroad.

Sighing, she put the half-eaten bowl of stew aside. There was no way to know exactly how they'd ended up here. Or how their captor knew Landon's identity.

Just as she decided that, the door to her room opened to reveal the guard who had escorted her to this part of the sprawling house. He indicated that she should come with him, stepping back from the doorway to allow her room to walk by him and into the hall.

She hadn't forgotten her captor's lesson about delays in following his instructions. Of course, she'd always been a quick learner. As long as he had Landon under his control, she was determined to give him no reason to punish him for her mistakes.

She rose, smoothing her hands down the front of the tunic the women had provided. Made of pale blue cotton, it was long and narrow, with a high neck and sleeves that fell partway over the backs of her hands. Under it she wore loose, matching trousers. A scarf in a darker blue had been laid out beside it, but she hadn't put it on. If it were important for wherever they were going, then surely her escort would send her back for it.

Instead, he turned as soon as she'd stepped out of the room, pulling the door closed behind her. He said something she didn't understand. When she looked back at him inquiringly, instead of repeating whatever the instruction had been, he prodded her between the shoulder blades with the muzzle of his weapon.

As good as words, she thought, stepping forward. Wherever he was taking her, maybe she would be allowed to see Landon again. Simply knowing she wasn't alone here would help her to bear whatever was to come.

Please, God.

IF HER CAPTOR was trying to intimidate her, he had succeeded. The huge room to which she'd been brought was elaborately furnished. The colors of the silk that had been hung at the windows and used as coverings for cushions on the floor were both rich and varied.

At the far end a massive chair, intricately carved and then gilded, had been set up on a low dais. Between that and the door through which she'd entered stretched what seemed to be a half mile of intricately patterned carpet.

On either side of that, the men who had participated in the ambush were seated on the floor, legs crossed, their eyes all on her. Their robes and turbans were now spotless, but the weapons they'd brandished yesterday lay across their laps.

Fat boy's throne room.

The thought was deliberately mocking. She was trying desperately not to let this display of power and wealth browbeat her. After all, her captor might be head honcho in this particular bit of desolate wilderness, but that's all he was. She, on the other hand, was a representative of the greatest nation on the face of the earth.

And it's thinking like that which makes half the world hate us.

Still, it was a reality she was determined to hold on to. Especially since she had so little else to cling to right now.

That wasn't true, either, she reminded herself. Landon was here. And there was no one she would be more willing to bet on in any kind of fight—even one that seemed as one-sided as this.

Besides, as he had told her from the start, a hell of a lot of people were working to find her. The most elite forces of the greatest military power the world had ever known.

And I hope that gives you a proper sense of inferiority, you fat bastard.

During her journey here, always conscious of the armed guard behind her, she'd been trying to remember everything she'd ever read about the psychology of the treatment of prisoners. On both sides of that equation.

This whole setup was exactly what she'd thought before—an attempt to intimidate her. Everything from the silent, seated army to the guard at her back to that huge, empty chair.

As if that thought had been a signal, one of the tribesmen pulled aside a silken curtain behind the "throne," allowing her captor to enter the room. The garb he'd worn yesterday had apparently been some kind of field uniform.

Today he was arrayed in a yellow silk robe over a red tunic that had been generously cut to disguise his bulk. Matching trousers had been tucked into a pair of lambskin boots. His turban was a darker shade of the material from which the outer robe was fashioned. Although she couldn't see his hands, she would be willing to bet they were heavily adorned with jewelry.

As the fat man seated himself, he adjusted the long robe so that it draped appropriately. Only then did he look up.

Finally he gestured with a Queen Elizabeth twist of his wrist. Grace wasn't sure if that was directed at her or her guard, but once more the muzzle of his weapon in contact with her spine left no doubt about what she was supposed to do.

Taking a deep breath, she began to walk down the

carpet. Although she refused to look anywhere but at the man who waited at the end of it, she was aware that the eyes of the men seated on either side followed her progress.

Let them look, she thought, her chin inching up a fraction. *Let them look their fill.*

As she neared the dais, she saw that the man seated there was watching her with a slight smile on his lips. A wave of anger, as strong as that she'd felt yesterday, washed over her.

Enjoy the show, you bastard. Believe me, it's going to cost you more than you can imagine.

"Ms. Chancellor."

The fat man inclined his head as if he really were granting her an audience. She expected him to hold out that damn ruby for her to kiss.

Dream on.

"How charming of you to join us. I assume your accommodations are to your satisfaction."

"The women who attended me were very kind." She'd be damned if she would thank him for holding her prisoner.

"Indeed?" He sounded surprised. And then he added, "I shall speak to them."

Obviously not to compliment them on their behavior. She wished she'd chosen any other remark than that, but it was too late to mitigate the damage she had done. She swallowed hard, her lips closing over her natural inclination to defend them. If she said nothing else, perhaps he would forget to carry out that threat. After all, he had more important things to think about.

As she worried about what he might do to the women, the smile she'd glimpsed between the oiled beard and mustache had widened. He was obviously enjoying this, she realized.

Despite her attempts to keep her spirits up, he clearly had the upper hand. And after yesterday, she knew he would not hesitate to use it. She could only try not to do or say anything that would give him an excuse to demonstrate his power.

"I'm sure you're wondering what has become of Mr. James."

"Of course."

There was no need to lie about that. He wouldn't have believed her in any case.

"Would you like to see him?"

There was something about the tone of that which caused the hair on the back of her neck to stir. Something…diabolical. Gloating.

"Or perhaps I've been misinformed about your relationship."

"Since I have no idea what information you've been given, or by whom, I can't say whether or not you've been misinformed. However, I would very much like to see Mr. James."

She almost added something about Landon's condition the last time she'd seen him, but caught the words back at the last second. There was no reason to allow this man to take more satisfaction in his cruelty than was absolutely necessary.

"Then you don't deny your relationship?"

"As I said, since I have no idea what you believe the

nature of that relationship to be…" Deliberately she let the sentence trail.

"That you were his whore. Do you deny that?"

She could feel the flush of color in her throat, but it was created by fury rather than the embarrassment he expected. She had no cause to feel the latter. Certainly not over her relationship with Landon, however this man might characterize it. She knew very well how Landon felt about her—

She had known, she realized with a blaze of insight that shocked her. She had always known that he'd loved her. And nothing this bastard could say could change that.

"Perhaps your understanding of the word is flawed," she said. "English is such a difficult language for foreigners."

For a moment the same cold enmity she'd seen yesterday replaced the amusement in those black eyes. He controlled it with an effort, forcing his mouth into a semblance of the smile it had worn before her challenge.

"Or perhaps it's *your* understanding of your situation that's flawed. If I may enlighten you…"

He nodded at someone behind her. Grace refused to look around, assuming his gesture had been another order to the guard who'd escorted her here.

She tried to brace herself for whatever "enlightenment" her intemperate tongue had just earned. Despite scoring high on the Agency's stress profiles, she had always wondered how well she would be able to stand up to physical or psychological torture. She prayed she wasn't about to find out.

"Ms. Chancellor?"

She looked up into the eyes of her captor, acknowledging that her momentary inattention, while understandable in light of his threat, had been foolish. She would need every bit of intellect and courage she possessed in order to endure whatever he had planned for her.

"I believe you expressed a wish to see Mr. James."

The fat man inclined his head toward the door through which she'd entered. Grace tried to steel herself to deny him the reaction he so clearly wanted to evoke.

The worst would be the sight of Landon's lifeless body. And then, remembering the stories of atrocities that were so casually committed in this part of the world, she knew there were a thousand things that would be more terrible than that.

She swallowed, trying to unobtrusively draw air into lungs that seemed to be frozen with horror. Whatever was behind her, she knew that she had no choice but to do her captor's bidding. After all, he could forcibly make her turn around. And for her own sake, she needed to maintain the pretence that she had some control of her actions as long as she could.

She turned, her heart once more crowding her throat. At first she couldn't quite grasp what she was seeing. And then, when she had, she was forced to blink to clear the tears that, unbidden, sprang to her eyes.

Chapter Fifteen

In the open doorway at the end of the patterned carpet, Landon stood between two guards. His hands were tied in front of him, the leather that bound them looped once around his neck. One of the guards held the end of it like a leash.

She searched Landon's face, looking for signs of abuse besides yesterday's bruises and abrasions. The single dark eye was locked on hers, but she could read nothing of what he was feeling or thinking there. It seemed as cold and lifeless as those of the man on the throne behind her.

He was dressed in a clean white tunic and matching trousers. Over them was one the traditional Afghani sleeveless weskits. It appeared he had at least had the luxury of a bath and fresh clothing.

That was all she could be sure of. If he'd been tortured—

"Would you care to make the introductions, Mr. James? Something we didn't have time for yesterday, I'm afraid."

There was a split second of hesitation, and then Landon said. "Grace, this is Abdul Rahim."

It was a name that would be familiar to anyone who knew this region. Although their captor was frequently referred to as a warlord, it was in the opium trade that he had acquired both his wealth and whatever standing he had in this society.

Landon's tone as he'd said the name had been flat, apparently free of emotion. She knew him well enough, however, to know that her earlier speculations had been correct. Landon and Abdul Rahim were old acquaintances and undoubtedly old enemies, as well.

"Politeness demands that one also provide some identifying information. Perhaps you'd care to try once more."

Although Abdul Rahim's words were delivered in the manner of a parent correcting a child or a teacher instructing a student, it was clear they contained a threat. One Landon would have no choice but to respond to.

"Abdul Rahim is the…ruler of this province. As was his father before him. He was educated at Eton and Cambridge and returned to Afghanistan to take the reins of government from his father's hands."

After he murdered him.

Landon didn't say that, of course, but it was in the intelligence material she had studied after learning of her reassignment: The man had, naturally, never gone to trial for that crime, but his guilt was widely assumed. Certainly at the CIA.

"And what can you tell me about Ms. Chancellor? I

understand that you two are intimately acquainted, although she objected quite strenuously to my characterization of your relationship."

"Ms. Chancellor is a senior analyst with the Central Intelligence Agency and formerly its assistant deputy director in charge of Middle Eastern Affairs."

"Formerly? But how unfortunate. My sympathies, Ms. Chancellor. And her current position?"

Again there was a slight hesitation. Grace turned to face her captor, deciding that he'd played puppet master long enough.

"I've been assigned to eradicate the processing of the opium poppy into heroin in Afghanistan and its distribution beyond its borders. I'm sure you're already aware of that."

"And you intend to speak for Mr. James? In our culture, women are silent unless they are spoken to."

"In our culture, whoever is most closely involved in the situation, and therefore the best informed, answers the questions. I'm sorry if I offended you."

Abdul Rahim laughed. "If there's one thing I'm very sure you are *not,* Ms. Chancellor, it's sorry to have offended me. However, since I was exposed to your customs while at school, I'm well aware of the behavior of Western women. I shall attempt to be tolerant of yours. After all, I'm sure you're under an enormous amount of stress right now."

"Really? And why should you assume that?"

"Because whatever else you may be, you're not a fool. And therefore you know that the task you've been given is intended to make you appear foolish."

There was nothing she could say to that. It was only the truth, bluntly stated.

"Ms. Chancellor has friends who will pay a great deal of money to have her safely returned to Kabul."

The fat man's laughter this time was so loud and prolonged that several of his lieutenants joined in. Their titters appeared almost nervous in comparison.

Grace doubted any of them had understood enough of Landon's offer to know why their leader was laughing. Apparently they had found it was politic to emulate his mood, whatever it was.

"Do I strike you as someone who is in need of money, Mr. James?"

"No matter how much money one has, one can always find a use for more," Landon said calmly.

She wondered if Griff had authorized him to make this kind of open-ended offer. Although the head of the Phoenix was said to be incredibly wealthy, she didn't know if he would be willing or able to provide the kind of bribe she feared Abdul Rahim would require to let them go.

Except, Landon hadn't attempted to bargain for his own release, she realized. The offer had been made only on her behalf.

And if you think I'm going to let you get away with that—

"I believe I prefer to hold on to Ms. Chancellor," Abdul Rahim said. "After all, I have a vested interest in seeing that her mission here fails."

"If it does, they'll send someone else to replace me," Grace said.

"And are there then so many people out of favor with your employer, Ms. Chancellor?"

He knew far more than he should. Perhaps he could have deduced that she was being punished simply by reading the American papers. That didn't explain, however, how he knew about her former relationship with Landon, something very few people were privy to, even among those who had worked with them at the Agency during that time.

"The State Department believes that the production and transportation of heroin from this country must be stopped. They'll do everything in their power to see that happen."

"Why should anyone in your country care what we do in ours? I have given the sovereignty of this province neither to the United States nor the Afghani government. And I never shall."

"Heroin funds terrorism. My government has sworn to eradicate that. You may be familiar with some of the recent…enterprises they have undertaken to that end."

It wouldn't help to remind him of their previous successes. Even if his ego was as huge as she suspected, he must know that he couldn't win any kind of war with the United States.

But maybe he can win the occasional battle…

She wondered briefly if her death at the hands of this madman would provoke an official retaliation. Or, as Landon had suggested earlier, would people at the top of the Agency take it as cause to celebrate.

"Eradicate terrorism, as well as *all* the poppies in Afghanistan? Your government has delusions of grandeur, my dear. I'm tempted to send you back to them with that message."

In spite of knowing he had no intention of sending her anywhere, there was a momentary surge of longing for the normality of her life before she'd been summoned to testify to the joint intelligence committees. Of course, the stress she'd endured during the last six months, worrying over her position at the Agency and her reputation, seemed ridiculous compared to the life-and-death situations she'd faced since the chopper had gone done.

Perspective. Everything was a matter of perspective.

"An excellent idea," Landon said. "One that's in everyone's best interest."

"Even *yours*? I'm surprised, given how close you and Ms. Chancellor are, that you would say that."

"Ms. Chancellor has nothing to do with your feelings toward me."

"Nor are *you* a fool, Mr. James. Please don't act like one."

"She's a bureaucrat. And you're well aware, as are the people at the CIA who sent her here, that whatever policies she initiates will have little effect on your business. After all, you operated quite efficiently under the Taliban."

"Because they were ignorant swine."

"As are those who assigned Ms. Chancellor this task," Landon said. "Your quarrel is with them."

"My quarrel, as you so simplistically put it, is with *you*."

"Then let Ms. Chancellor—"

"And there is no sweeter revenge on one's enemy than to make him suffer vicariously."

The sudden silence was thick enough to smell. Or maybe that was the scent of her own fear.

...to make him suffer vicariously. There was only one possible interpretation of that.

"You must be aware—" Landon began again, his voice still calm, only to be cut off once more.

"Your arguments bore me. *You* bore me. The first time we met, you escaped my anger. Not entirely unscathed, of course. Does she make you turn out the lights when she makes love to you now?"

She knew Landon wouldn't answer that. No man would. And even though their current relationship had not included the kind of intimacy Abdul Rahim suggested, she also knew from Landon's reaction when she'd touched the patch that covered his eye, that in spite of his normal arrogance, there would be some part of him that had wondered the same thing.

"No, she doesn't," Grace said. "Actually, I wonder why you would think of that. I would guess that might be a personal observation about the squeamishness of women, but then it's an expedience that really wouldn't work in your case, would it?"

Since she was going to be tortured or killed to make Landon suffer, then there seemed little use in holding back her feelings about this bastard. She'd had to bite her tongue often enough with those back in Washington. And look where it had gotten her.

"Are you hinting that you'd enjoy testing your theory, my dear? That can be arranged, I assure you. I don't suppose Mr. James would enjoy the thought of our copulation."

"Nor would I," Grace said.

"You might be surprised."

The fat man seemed more amused than angered at her attempts to ridicule him. Perhaps because of all those in this room, only the three of them were fluent enough in English to follow the conversation.

"If you know as much as you claim," Landon said, "then you must be aware that until the last few days in this country, Ms. Chancellor and I haven't set eyes on one another in more than seven years. Hardly the kind of relationship you believe we enjoyed."

"*Once* enjoyed," Abdul Rahim said. "There is, however, apparently enough feeling on your part that you would travel halfway around the world to rescue her."

"What makes you think I came to Afghanistan for that reason?"

"Are you suggesting there was another?"

The slight smile Grace had noticed before was back on the thick lips. Apparently his good humor had been restored by whatever Landon was saying.

"A friend pulled some strings in Washington so I could get back into the region. The powers that be had feared I might have some…personal agenda in coming here. A vendetta that could cause problems for their plans."

"How astute of them."

"Remarkably so, considering that they've had no real clue as to what was going on in this region during the last twenty years."

Abdul Rahim's laughter was unforced this time, seeming to be generated by a genuine amusement rather than by any attempt to harass or belittle them. Grace didn't understand why the dynamics had changed, but the sense of threat had definitely lessened.

"So Ms. Chancellor's abduction simply provided you a vehicle by which you might come back to my country for another visit. I'm flattered, I assure you."

"Obviously, this isn't the situation I had envisioned."

"No, I should imagine not. Especially with the complication Ms. Chancellor represents."

"This has always been between you and me. Let her go."

"How chivalric. However, I find that there is a certain piquancy in having your paramour under my control. Even if you no longer have feelings for her—and frankly, with your spirited defense, I have my doubts about that—there's a certain satisfaction in taking a woman you once made love to."

"I can't imagine what that would be. She's a woman. That's all she ever was to me. To the U.S. Government, however, she's far more. If you harm her, they'll hunt you down, and you know it. The only excuse they'll need is stored in the buildings of this very village. No one is going to question if they decided to take out a man of your reputation."

"They would have to find me first."

Landon laughed, the sound short and mocking. "If they want to, they could put a rocket into your toilet. While you're on it."

"Which explains their long hunt for Osama, I suppose."

"You aren't Osama. There are too many people who wouldn't mind seeing you put out of business. Your competitors. Ms. Chancellor's replacement. The government in Kabul."

"That may be so, but none of them have succeeded yet."

"Perhaps because you haven't yet given them an adequate reason to mount a campaign against you. Kill Grace Chancellor, and I promise you that campaign will be launched."

As if to punctuate the threat Landon had just made, an explosion rocked the building, to be quickly followed by others outside. After their initial shock, the tribesmen who had been seated on either side of the carpet were on their feet, weapons in hand, a babble of inquiry underlying the continued bombardment of the compound.

Grace turned, her eyes locking on Landon's in the midst of the hubbub. Where there had been only bleakness before, there seemed to be a gleam of satisfaction within its dark depths.

The guard on his right had tightened his hold on the leash, but he seemed as confused about what to do as the rest. And then the voice of the man at the front of the room cut through the disorder like a scythe.

Grace understood nothing of the commands he issued, but his forces responded immediately. Those who had been seated with their weapons began to pour out through the entrance where she and Landon had entered.

Landon's keeper led him to the side. The second one grabbed her arm, pulling her over beside them.

"What the hell?" she asked as soon as she was close enough to speak to him.

"I've been telling you they're looking for you."

Special Forces? It had to be, she realized. And like some avenging army, they were just in the nick of time. Of course, considering everything that had gone wrong since she'd been in the country, it was about time. With all the images from the spy satellites that were available to them, she was only surprised it had taken them this long to find her.

Abdul Rahim's desire to get Landon had obviously led him to make a fatal error. That precisely planned ambush she'd admired would have been recorded on those pictures. Obviously someone had recognized him, maybe from his size alone. And now her government, with whose power she had attempted to comfort herself, had come after him.

I told you that you were messing with the wrong people.

Abdul Rahim was still issuing orders, and apparently these had to do with their disposition. They were hustled out of the building without ceremony and into the dark compound, where the ferociousness of the attack was made quickly apparent.

A C130 gunship, affectionately known as a "Spooky," circled overhead, a deadly barrage of firepower raining down on the village from its laser-guided armament. Even as some part of her celebrated its effectiveness as a killing machine, Grace realized that outside and in the darkness, she and Landon were as vulnerable to its weapons as were Abdul Rahim and his men.

Chapter Sixteen

All he needed was a chance, Landon thought as, prodded by the guns of the tribesmen, they ran across the compound. A momentary inattention on the part of his guard that would allow him to somehow get Grace out of the control of hers.

Whatever happened now, Landon knew this would be his *last* chance. The last opportunity to save Grace from what Abdul Rahim had planned. The last chance to save them both. Surely to God, in the midst of this chaos—

A shell from the C130's howitzer struck within a few feet of Grace and her escort, close enough that it sent up a mushroom cloud of debris. While rocks and clods of dirt rained back down on all of them, Landon saw that the aftershock had hit with enough force to knock Grace to her knees. Her guard bent to drag her up, automatically raising his other arm, the one with which he held his automatic weapon, to act as a shield between him and the fallout from the explosion.

Landon glanced behind him. The second man, who was supposed to be guarding him, was instead watching the scene playing out in front of them.

Last chance, echoed in Landon's brain.

He took a couple of running steps to the side, raising his joined hands as high as he could. The second guard looked around as Landon began to move, but by then it was far too late.

The tribesman had time to recognize that he was being attacked, but not enough to prevent the assault already in motion. When Landon's hands reached the apex of their upward swing, he brought them down and across, slamming his lead elbow into the man's face.

The blow caught him in the nose, just as Landon had intended. Despite the shrieks of the village women and the rattle of the Spooky's Gatling guns, he clearly heard bone snap.

If he'd struck in exactly the right place, the blow should have driven that bone into the man's brain. If he hadn't…

Unwilling to risk the latter, Landon grabbed the guard's weapon with both hands, ripping it away as the man reeled backwards. He released Landon's lead to grab at his nose.

Knowing he couldn't get the gun into firing position with his wrists tied together and his hands numbed by the tightness of his bonds, Landon didn't even try to turn the weapon, but jammed the stock under the man's raised chin. Although the guard was already falling away, Landon again felt a solid connection, the AK-47 reverberating within his leaden palms.

Without waiting for his adversary to hit the ground, he started forward, awkwardly trying to reverse the weapon as he ran so that he could swing it like a club.

By now Grace's escort had gotten her to her feet. Despite the continuing bombardment of the compound, the man glanced back to check on his companion.

Even in the darkness Landon could see his eyes widen as he realized the situation. Whether his shock would last long enough for Landon to close the distance between them would be too close to call.

He completed the back swing with the weapon he'd stolen as he sprinted across the last few feet that separated him from Grace's guard, who was frantically trying to get his own gun into firing position. Forcing out of his mind the thought of what that powerful semiautomatic would do if his adversary *did* manage to get it up, Landon concentrated instead on reaching the man before he could.

A fraction of a second before the guard's finger closed around the trigger Landon knew he'd failed. At the same instant he had reached that bitter realization, Grace lunged full-out for the muzzle of the AK-47.

With her outstretched fingertips, she shoved the barrel aside as she fell. A stream of bullets plowed the ground almost at Landon's feet, close enough that he could feel their impact.

And then he was there, the stock of the weapon he carried thudding into the side of the guard's head with a resounding crack, as if someone had broken open an overripe melon. The man went down, his finger still locked on the trigger of the AK-47, which continued to spray bullets into the air.

For the first time since the errant shell had provided the distraction he'd been praying for, Landon had the luxury of a relatively threat-free moment to focus on Grace. Although she was lying prone, he saw no visible injury. No bloodstains marred the tunic she wore or the ground beneath her.

He bent, preparing to help her up without putting down the weapon he'd stolen, something he was reluctant to do. That decision was suddenly taken out of his hands when it became apparent that the Spooky's electronic surveillance equipment had detected movement in this area of the compound. The powerful Gatling guns were now churning up dirt in a line headed straight toward their position.

He grabbed Grace's elbow, trying to pull her to her feet. "Come on."

Instead of obeying, she jerked away, scrambling on her hands and knees to where the guard lay on the blood-soaked ground. She seemed to be searching his body. Whatever she was doing, Landon thought, his eyes flicking up to gauge the approaching firestorm, they didn't have time for.

"Run, damn it," he screamed, grabbing her elbow and using it to jerk her up.

This time she obeyed, following him as he sprinted toward the entrance to the low bunkerlike building where the guards had been taking them. He hoped Abdul Rahim's fortifications were as invulnerable to attack as they were purported to be.

He elbowed open the door and then waited for Grace to stumble through it. Her boots were clattering over the concrete stairs before he himself dived through, pulling the steel door closed behind him with only seconds to spare. Bullets from the C130's guns followed, beating a tattoo up the door and across the roof.

Panting, he followed Grace down the stairs, the semi-automatic held awkwardly in his bound hands. As he descended into the almost total blackness of the underground bunker, he began to realize that, remarkably, he was not only alive, but untouched. As for Grace…

"Grace," he hissed at the bottom of the stairs, unsure with whom they might be sharing the bunker.

Instead of answering, she touched his hand, her trembling fingers wrapping around his. He closed his eyes in relief, feeling the unaccustomed sting of tears at the back of them.

"Be still," she whispered, leaning against him so that her lips were against his ear.

He froze, expecting the worst. Then her fingers traced across the back of his hand until they found the leather binding his wrists. Only when he felt the strong downward pressure on it did he understand what she'd been doing when she crawled over to the guard he'd downed.

Grace had taken the long, curved knife the tribesman had worn on his belt, something she'd obviously noticed when they were inside the fat man's "palace." Now she was using its razor-sharp blade to saw through his bonds.

Like her deflection of the automatic weapon, her forethought in this was the kind of thing that might make the difference between success and failure. Literally, in this situation, between life and death.

For someone untrained in fieldwork, her actions

throughout their escape had been not only courageous but brilliant. He'd always known how bright Grace was, but he'd assumed her intellect was a kind more suited to the analysis at which she'd excelled during her years with the Agency. Now he knew she was someone he could count on in a very different type of crisis.

He waited, unable to help, as she worked. Although the darkness was too solid to determine without any doubt that they were alone, he could hear nothing inside the bunker but the sound of their still-ragged breathing and the steady whisper of the moving blade.

Outside, the C130 continued to pound the compound. Whatever weaponry Abdul Rahim's men had, and Landon had no doubt they were well equipped, they couldn't hope to touch that electronically protected "ghost," flying high above their heads.

He felt the leather part. As Grace began to unwind it from around his wrists, the blood flowing into his hands caused him to bow his head against the agony. He locked his teeth in his lower lip, fighting against any outward expression of it.

Before the pain had passed, Grace's hands fastened on either side of his face, lifting it. In the darkness, her mouth closed over his.

Her lips were cold and, like her hands, they trembled. Surprised by their first almost tentative touch, it had taken him a second to react. Then his arm closed hard around her, dragging her against his chest, as his mouth began to devour hers. Claiming what had always been his. Reclaiming what, through his stupidity, he had once thrown away as if it had been worth nothing to him.

Her response was immediate, her hunger as great as his. From long experience, he understood that was a reaction to the realization they were both alive, when only minutes before it had seemed they couldn't be. Maybe part of this was also because she had realized her long ordeal was almost over. But at least some of her reaction, he was convinced, was the result of the same sense of absolute rightness he felt at having her again in his arms.

Another of the howitzer's shells exploded outside the door of the reinforced bunker. Grace's lips broke contact with his, but she ducked her head, burrowing it against his chest. He tightened his hold around her body until the resulting reverberation had died away.

"Since *they're* up there, doesn't that mean they have to know we're down here?" she asked.

"Except, from where they are, we look like everyone else in the village."

Shadowy, antlike movements on a radar screen.

He could tell by the sounds filtering in from outside that Abdul Rahim's forces were starting to mount a resistance. Although he knew they possessed shoulder-to-air antiaircraft missiles, either taken from the Soviets or obtained on the black market, he wasn't too worried.

The Spooky's electronic shielding would protect it from anything other than a random hit. And as high as the plane could circle and still conduct its killing bombardment, there was no one down here who would get that lucky tonight.

"But…you *do* think they're looking for us?"

Or carrying out someone's orders, maybe those of Grace's successor, to hit the opium dealers where it would hurt most—in their warehouses and transport hubs. Still, with as many people as were supposedly searching for Grace, it was entirely possible that someone had finally gotten off his lazy, bureaucratic ass and managed to buy some accurate intel.

Possible, he thought with the cynicism of long experience, *but I'll be damned if I'm going to count on it.*

"You leave any orders to strike the drug dealers on your desk in Kabul?" he asked, deliberately imbuing the question with a hint of amusement.

"I didn't have time to *locate* my desk. I'm not sure they had even provided me with one."

"Then maybe they've already replaced you."

"Or *maybe*," she said, countering his determined negativism, "someone looked at the satellite images and figured out where we are."

"Or maybe we're still on our own."

If this was a drug raid rather than a rescue, there was no guarantee that the Special Forces would follow the C130's strike. Maybe the gunship had been sent here to destroy the warehouses and the processing plant. Maybe this attack had nothing at all to do with them, other than some kind of retaliation for Grace's kidnapping.

"What does that mean?"

"That I'm not sure we can count on boots on the ground as part of this assault."

"But…that's what the C130 does. Provides air support for a ground operation."

Trust Grace to know. And she was right, of course. It was just that Landon had learned through the years not to count on anyone but himself. An old lesson that he believed was still as valid as the day he'd first mastered it.

"Not always. And I'm not willing to wait until that plane up there turns for home to find out whether that's what they're doing or not."

They had left the bodies of their guards in the middle of the compound. As soon as the C130 was no longer on patrol above it, Abdul Rahim's men would find them. When they did, the search would be on. And the last place they should be then was where they were now.

"So…what do we do?"

"We get the hell out of here."

"On foot?"

"That's the safest way."

Unless they wanted to start searching for some vehicle in which someone had left the keys or for one old enough that he could hotwire it. He had no doubt there would be one or the other around here, but he didn't want to try to find it with the C130 circling above them and Abdul Rahim's men on his tail.

Far better to get away from the compound under the cover of darkness. Then, if Grace were right about the Special Forces moving in, they could come back down at daylight and make contact with them.

"You mean…just leave? Without water? Or transportation?" Each phrase had been separate, articulated as she fully comprehended what his suggestion entailed.

Of course, he was the one intimately familiar with the fat man's idea of hospitality. Dying of dehydration was preferable to the kind of fun and games Abdul Rahim had in store for them. Far preferable.

"If you're right," he said, "it will only be a couple of hours until we can come back."

If the Special Forces had been dispatched to the village to search for Grace, they would know by first light. Despite his cynicism, he hoped like hell she was right. There could be nothing that would excite him more right now than seeing a couple of dozen U.S. Rangers show up down here.

It just wasn't something he was willing to count on.

Chapter Seventeen

As they had picked their way up the mountainside in the darkness, they had listened to the continuing gunfire from the village they'd left behind. They had climbed for perhaps half an hour before they found the cave where they had eventually taken shelter.

Judging by the sounds of the battle below, however, Abdul Rahim wasn't going to have an opportunity to mount a search for the two of them anytime soon. He had more important concerns. And with the confusion inherent in this kind of attack, he might not even be aware yet that his prisoners were missing.

The only danger Landon could see in hiding on the mountainside until the fireworks were over was the possibility the C130 had been sent to hit the heroin processing operation rather than to provide air support for search and rescue. Even if that were the case, it still made more sense to him for Grace to be here and not in the village. He was willing to risk not making contact with a rescue team to avoid the chance of Grace being recaptured by that sadistic bastard.

"That's *not* the C130," she whispered.

The gunfire from below was different now. Short bursts from automatic weaponry were followed by relatively long periods of silence. A pattern that seemed to indicate someone was moving from building to building, systematically taking control of each.

"I think there's an assault team on the ground."

"Then we need to get back down there before they leave," Grace urged, gripping his arm.

"It's too dangerous right now."

"But…what if they leave without us?"

"If they're searching for you, they won't. Not before sunrise, at least. This isn't some prisoner snatch being carried out in a hostile country, remember. This is territory *we* control.

"Maybe in *theory*. You know how far from reality that is."

"If they've been sent to find you, they aren't going anywhere until they're sure you're not there," he reiterated. "But if this is some kind of retaliatory drug raid, you'd be in as much danger in that village right now as Abdul Rahim's men are. Actually, you'd be in greater danger. After all, his plans for you were interrupted by this. I'm sure he'd be thrilled to have you back under his control."

The threat shut her up, if only momentarily. Given his own questions as to whether this was the wisest course, Landon supposed he'd have to be satisfied with her silence. He wished it were as easy to quiet his own demons of doubt.

"Is that what happened before? You were under his control?"

"Most people don't live through mistakes of that magnitude. Unfortunately, I did."

"'Unfortunately'?"

He had said too much. And he had no explanation for why. After years of keeping what had happened on that last mission locked inside, he had just revealed far more than he'd told anyone about it. Even Griff. And he'd revealed it to the one person whose opinion mattered even more to him than that of the head of the External Security Team.

"Whatever happened…" Grace began and then hesitated. "*Everybody* has a breaking point, Landon. No matter how brave or how tough you are, there's a point at which no one can resist torture. We learned that from Vietnam. Actually, we knew it long before 'Nam, but since then we've officially acknowledged the existence of that limit."

"Is that supposed to make me feel better?"

He sounded like a child. Or a fool. It didn't matter to anyone how he felt about what had happened to him. Not "officially" or any other way.

"Is that why you left the Agency?"

It was, of course, but probably not in the way she meant. The loss of his eye and the other injuries he'd suffered had simply given him a legitimate excuse for resigning. They hadn't really been the reason he'd done so.

"I left because I didn't feel I could be an effective operative any longer." That, too, was part of the truth.

"I doubt Griff agreed with that assessment."

"It wasn't Griff's decision."

"Maybe not, but… I know he wanted you for the

Phoenix. If he had thought you weren't capable of doing the job—"

"Let it go, Grace. It really *doesn't* matter. Not any more."

"But it *was* Abdul Rahim, wasn't it? He's the one who did that to you."

She meant the loss of his eye. And she was right, of course. As traumatic as that had been, Abdul Rahim's threat to remove the other had been far worse. One of the many forms of psychological torture he'd employed.

Landon swallowed the rush of bile into his throat, remembering terrors he didn't want to remember. Images he had steadfastly refused for years to let allow back into his head.

Except in his nightmares. Those he hadn't been able to control.

Griff had urged him to talk to one of the CIA's psychiatrists. He probably should have, but he'd known even then that no matter what mumbo-jumbo they would come up with to explain what he'd done to stay alive, it wouldn't change what had happened. Nothing could.

"Why? Why you? Why him?"

"I passed the word to the Pakistani authorities about a shipment he was sending over the Pass. They confiscated it, of course, but like almost everything else around here, the information about who had tipped them off was apparently for sale. Finding out my name and location cost Abdul Rahim much less than he had lost on the shipment. In any case, he seemed to think he'd gotten a bargain."

"He wanted retribution for what he'd lost."

"At first. And then…" He took a breath, again fighting those nightmare images. "And then it got personal. It still is."

"And *he's* the reason you came back." Her voice was low and flat. Without emotion.

She wouldn't believe a denial. Why should she? Besides, she deserved the truth. At least as much of it as he could tell.

"What Griff asked you to do…" she went on. "Finding me. That was just an excuse to return."

His motives in coming back to Afghanistan were so complicated by what had happened on that last mission, he knew he couldn't explain them to her. And in trying to make her understand, he also knew he would hurt her. Something he'd never intended to do.

The truth was that he *had* come here to find Grace. And to get her safely out of the country. But again, that was only part of the truth. The rest was between him and Abdul Rahim.

Personal.

"But if you were so determined to find him—" She stopped, obviously figuring it all out as she went. "They restricted your passport so you *couldn't* come back. God, that sounds like something those bastards would do."

They both understood that the State Department wasn't worried about protecting him. It was the possibility of having a rogue agent on the loose in Afghanistan, an agent with a personal agenda and a thirst for revenge, they had tried to prevent.

"After 9/11 Abdul Rahim was smart enough to see the writing on the wall. Suddenly—and at a time when the Agency desperately needed one—he became a highly reliable source of information about the activities of the Taliban and their forces. Whatever…enmity there was between us very quickly became secondary to that concern."

As it should have been. Besides…

"So when Griff asked you to find me," Grace said, "you jumped at the chance to come back and confront him. And the friend with the truck?" she went on. "The one who was going to take us into Pakistan? Did he ever exist? Or was that just part of the plan to get you here?"

"You know me better than that, Grace. I would never intentionally involve you with someone like Abdul Rahim."

"So…you were going to take me into Pakistan and then what?"

"After I had put you on a plane to Washington, I was going to come back across the mountains."

Just get her on a plane and out of his life again. That *had* been his original intent. At least until he'd seen her.

"So the encounter with Reynolds, Abdul Rahim's ambush… You're saying you set none of that into motion?"

"My intent was exactly what I told you. Come in through Pakistan and take you back out the same way. Everything went wrong, almost from the first."

"And now? If those *are* Special Forces down there, Landon, what's the plan now?"

"I'm going to do what I promised Griff. I'm going to put you into their very capable hands."

"And then you're going after Abdul Rahim. What makes you think that he'll still be there? He's a bully, and most bullies are cowards. He won't stay to fight. He may order his men to, but he'll be gone long before dawn."

The anger in her voice had been replaced at the last by something that sounded like triumph. Except she was wrong, of course. Not about her assessment of Abdul Rahim, but about the effectiveness of the plan of attack.

"Nobody's getting out of that village tonight. Not with that C130 patrolling overhead. You saw how quickly the equipment honed in on our movement. If Abdul Rahim attempts to leave, he'll be signing his own death warrant."

"Good," Grace said, the anger back. "Then it will all be *over,* and you won't have to do a thing."

It won't ever be over. Not for me. Not unless I pull the trigger on that fat bastard myself.

"Promise me something," he said, realizing that he might be missing out on his last chance to do exactly that.

"Not until I know what it is."

"I want you to wait up here."

"While you go down there and try to find Abdul Rahim? If you show up down there now, looking like you do, you're just another of his men to that assault team."

"That's a chance I'm willing to take."

"But I'm *not* willing to let you take it."

"Grace—"

"I'm your passport, Landon. I'm your safe passage down there. The only one you've got. If they *are* looking for me, they aren't going to shoot first and ask questions later. And even if they aren't, I think they'll recognize me. After all, there can't be too many 'ice maidens' roaming around in this part of the world."

"That's insane." Despite his denial, he found he was thinking about it.

"I'm your ticket to Abdul Rahim. You know it and I know it. If we go down there together, we kill two birds with one stone. I end up in the hands of coalition forces, which is what you promised Griff, and you have your chance at him."

"It's too dangerous."

"Yeah? Well, so is blood poisoning."

The non sequitur threw him. Then, when he remembered her injury, a trickle of cold moved through his stomach.

"What does that mean?"

She took his hand, putting it just above the bandage he'd wound around her arm. Even through the material, he could feel the swelling and the heat radiating from her skin.

Inflammation. Infection. Blood poisoning. The same deadly progression that had killed Mike Mitchell. And if they missed making contact with the Special Forces unit he believed was on the ground in Abdul Rahim's village…

"It's been less than forty-eight hours."

Not long enough for an infection to develop. Not nearly long enough, he told himself.

"Maybe those things in that first-aid kit were contaminated. Or maybe you didn't get out all the debris. I don't know. All I know is that since last night it's hurt like hell. Far more than it did when it happened."

That was to be expected, but still, he didn't like the hot swelling above the wound. He wished he could take a look at it, but to do that, he would have to wait until sunrise. And the stakes of that being the right decision had just been raised.

"Your choice, Landon. And time's running out for you to make it."

The very sound reasoning that had sent them scrambling up here and away from the attack no longer made sense. Now it seemed that Grace's best chance lay with those elite soldiers searching Abdul Rahim's stronghold.

As did his.

If the bastard was still alive, he was down there. And for the first time in a situation where the odds were not so overwhelmingly in his favor.

His men were occupied with the invaders. Abdul Rahim would have retreated to one of his secret bunkers deep in the mountain. Although he would still have his personal bodyguard around him, he would be vulnerable in a way he'd never before been in the course of their acquaintance.

"Landon?"

He nodded, so caught up in the anticipation of settling the score that he had forgotten she couldn't see the gesture. When he moved out of the entrance to the low cave, however, Grace followed.

Two birds with one stone, she had said. If he could again find his infamous luck, during the next few hours both of the missions he'd come to Afghanistan to carry out would be completed.

THE VILLAGE HAD BEEN eerily quiet as they approached. The scattered gunfire they'd heard earlier had faded as they made their descent, but smoke from the numerous fires the gunship had ignited hung over the low buildings like a pall.

Landon had left her hidden behind the rocks at the bottom of the slope as he'd moved slightly ahead to scout out the situation. She had watched until he disappeared, slipping like a ghost through the darkness. He was back in less than five minutes, easing down beside her as noiselessly as when he'd left.

"Rangers. And they're looking for you."

"You talked to them?"

He shook his head. "They're rounding up what's left of Abdul Rahim's men and questioning them in the center of the compound."

She didn't feel the elation she should in hearing the news. Instead, the same emptiness she'd experienced every morning during those terrible weeks after she'd issued her ultimatum settled like a cold stone in her chest.

Which was insane. No one could *want* to be on the run in Afghanistan. Certainly not in this wild and lawless region.

She turned her head, looking at Landon. In the flickering light from a burning truck, she could see the contusion at his temple. His unshaven cheeks seemed leaner because of their darkness, they and the black patch again making his appearance sinister. If she hadn't known him so well…

But she did. Intimately. As he had known her. With his hands and his mouth and his tongue. Nothing hidden. Nothing forbidden. And nothing ever forgotten.

"Why can't you let it go?" she asked.

"Could you?"

Of course, she thought. Of course.

That was the difference between them. Whatever Abdul Rahim had done—and she had no doubt, given the kind of man Landon was, it had been horrific— Landon had survived.

Now the possibility of so much happiness lay ahead. For both of them. All he had to do—

"We need to go."

He was anxious to get her off his hands. Anxious to turn her over to the Special Forces and let them take her back to Kabul and from there to the States. As for him...

"Come home with me."

She hadn't known those words were in her head before they were in her mouth. She didn't regret saying them. She hadn't begged before. She had gathered her pride instead, holding it before her like a shield as she'd presented her ultimatum.

And for seven empty years she had lived with the consequences. This time she at least didn't intend to be haunted by "What if..."

"I can't."

"Whatever he did to you—"

"Don't," he said softly.

It wasn't a command, but it had the force of one. The single word was edged with so much pain her eyes burned with tears she would never let him see her shed.

"It doesn't matter, Landon. Not to me."

"But it does to me."

She ached to touch him. To put her hand against his cheek. To pull that proud dark head down against her breasts and cradle it against her heart. And yet she knew he would hate nothing more than her pity.

"And when he's dead?" she asked. "Will you come to me then?"

He took a breath, deep enough to be audible in the predawn stillness. "If I can. But...if I can't, Grace..." His voice faded, so that he was forced to begin again. "If I can't, try to forgive me. And know there's nothing in this world I ever wanted more than that."

"Nothing except Abdul Rahim's death." Deliberately she let her bitterness show.

This was a choice. *His* choice. And again he hadn't chosen her. He had *never* chosen her.

"I've lived with this for five years. Why do you think I didn't contact you after I left the Agency?"

"Are you saying that...if it hadn't been for what happened here, you would have come to find me?"

"I didn't have to *find* you. There wasn't a day that went by that I didn't know where you were."

That was a confession she had never expected to hear. One that should have been a balm for the pain of those long, lonely years. Instead, it made her furious.

It hadn't been that he didn't love her enough. It hadn't been any of the things she had once believed. It had all centered on that fat bastard with his ruby rings and his perfumed beard and his yellow silk pajamas.

Whatever Abdul Rahim had done to Landon, she knew with a cold certainty she couldn't undo. Whatever she said would go unheard. He had already made up his mind about what he needed to do to be free. Knowing him as she did, she knew that nothing less would suffice.

And once again all she could do would be to wait.

THE FIRST FAINT LIGHT of dawn now touched the tops of the mountains, painting the deserted streets with a pale half-light.

"Stay close," Landon whispered, turning to glance at her over his shoulder.

She knew that for her these few minutes before they encountered the Special Forces were the most dangerous part of this. If they didn't recognize her, despite her coloring—

"Ms. Chancellor?" She turned at the sound of her name, finding a Ranger pointing his weapon at them, his face blackened for last night's raid.

"I'm Grace Chancellor," she said, raising her hands. "And I'd like to go home, please."

"Yes, ma'am. That's what we're here for." The muzzle of the weapon shifted its focus so that its line of sight was now centered on Landon's back. "Halt," the young soldier called, raising his voice enough to ensure the command would be heard.

Another couple of black-faced ghosts appeared from the alley behind him, the whites of their eyes bright in contrast to the greasepaint around them.

"That man's a friend," Grace said.

"We know who he is, Ms. Chancellor. If you'll just step aside, ma'am..."

"He has some business to attend to here."

"*Nobody* has any business here, ma'am. Not anymore. This village is now under the control of the coalition."

"Then you've captured Abdul Rahim?"

There had been a flutter of hope in her chest at the possibility, but the long silence that followed her question provided its answer. Despite her fear for the dangerous task Landon was determined to undertake, some small part of her rejoiced in the knowledge that there was still a chance he could do what he had said he had to do. To kill Abdul Rahim. And maybe then…

"We're still in the process of searching the buildings."

"You won't find what you're looking for. Abdul Rahim left the village just before the C130 arrived," she lied. "I don't know if he had prior warning or if it was just a coincidence, but…in any case, unless you are searching the surrounding area, I don't think you'll find him tonight."

The Ranger who had done all the talking so far glanced back at his companions. One responded with a quick lift of his shoulders.

"Get word upstairs," the first one ordered, sending the one who had shrugged off at a run.

"And now if you don't mind…" Grace said, "I really would like to go home."

Come home with me…

She had asked Landon something very much like that before. And just as he had tonight, he had turned her down to again put his life at risk. Then it had been for his country. Now…

Now it was personal. A score to settle.

Maybe when it had been, he would finally be free of

what had happened here five years ago. Free and whole again. If not in body, then in soul.

She turned, trying to locate him in the dimness of the smoke-filled street, but he had already disappeared. Another mission. Another death. And just as she had before, all she could do was to wait until it was over.

Chapter Eighteen

"And that's the last I saw of him. I don't even know if he found Abdul Rahim."

"Considering that the Rangers eventually discovered his body in a very well-equipped bunker in the mountain, one that was guarded by his personal bodyguards by the way, I would assume Landon had been there first."

Knowing Griff's connections within the intelligence community, Grace understood that his "assumption" probably came from field reports. That was undoubtedly how he had learned of Stern's survival, as well.

The attack she and Landon had heard during his original rescue attempt had been carried out by Special Forces assigned to look for the survivors of the Kiowa's crash. Colonel Stern had managed to connect with some of them during the following day.

According to Griff, as soon as he had described their rescuer to his debriefers, someone in intel had recognized the description of the man with the patch as possibly former CIA agent Landon James. From Landon's presence in Afghanistan to Abdul Rahim had been a leap of logic that even the current analysts had been able to make.

In any case, Landon's enemy was dead, and the commando team that had been sent in to find him and Grace hadn't brought Landon back with them. If they had, Griff would have told her that, too. Which meant Landon was probably even now using his knowledge of the area to work his way across the mountains into Pakistan.

"So he accomplished what he went to Afghanistan to do," she said aloud. "Maybe now…"

"Maybe now he can put those ghosts to rest," Griff finished when she hesitated.

"And maybe you'll get what you want, too." She smiled at the man seated across the big desk, whose eyes were too expressive of his concern.

Apparently, the emotional fragility she'd felt since her arrival back in Washington was more obvious than she'd believed. Or Griff was more observant than most of the people she'd encountered since her return.

She hadn't yet reported back to the Agency, but she had made up her mind about what she was going to do. One of the few decisions about which she'd had no doubts.

"Landon working as a member of the Phoenix, you mean?" Griff asked. "As much as I'd like that, I don't expect it to happen. I think he tired of this life a long time ago. Besides, he's made quite a name for himself as an international security consultant. I doubt he'd want to give up that kind of financial success to undertake the pro bono missions we're increasingly involved with. I'm simply grateful he agreed to undertake this one."

"This one was…personal," Grace said, remembering what she'd heard in Landon's voice.

"You're right. It was. But if you think Abdul Rahim was what drove him back to Afghanistan—"

"Don't," she said, unconsciously echoing Landon's warning to her. "I know you're trying to help. And believe me, I appreciate your concern, more than you can ever know, but… As a friend, Griff, just don't."

"Don't tell you that Landon *didn't* return to Afghanistan because of Abdul Rahim? Why? That's the truth."

"He jumped at the opportunity. And it wasn't because of me. Don't get me wrong. I'm grateful for what he did. And equally grateful to you for sending him."

She was. Considering the actions of her original captors and those of Steven Reynolds, it was likely that without Landon's intervention she would never have left Afghanistan alive.

"If Abdul Rahim had been Landon's primary motivation in going back, Grace, he would have made that journey long before now."

"The State Department restricted his passport."

Griff knew that, of course. He was the one who would have had to pull strings to get that restriction lifted.

"And you think that could have stopped an experienced operative as skilled and inventive as Landon James? With a border that porous, he could have gotten in anytime he wanted."

"Then…I don't understand. Why didn't he?"

Griff's assertion didn't fit with the need Landon had

expressed to her. The need to be free of those memories. A need he said could only be satisfied by Abdul Rahim's death.

"I don't know. Maybe he lacked an incentive."

"He had one. He wanted revenge. And believe me, in this case that would be incentive for almost anything."

Maybe Griff didn't understand what Abdul Rahim had done to Landon. Or the effect it had had on the man he'd once been.

"I think when he learned you were missing, he realized why it was so important to regain what he lost during that last mission."

"I don't know what I had to do with that."

"Why don't you ask him to explain it to you?"

Cabot opened his desk drawer and extracted a business card. He glanced at it before he slid it across the gleaming mahogany surface. Although she knew what would be on the small rectangle of cardboard, she made no effort to reach out and take it.

"I'd give him a few more days, if I were you," Griff said.

"I gave him seven years. It didn't make any difference."

"Maybe this time it will."

SHE HAD WAITED A WEEK, her heart rate accelerating every time the phone rang. Finally she took the card Griff had given her from her billfold.

Her initial impulse was to tear it into pieces so small she would be able to read neither the address nor the phone number it contained. That inclination was almost as compelling as the one that prompted her to study the bold black lettering instead until it was too late.

She would never forget anything that was printed there. Just as she had never forgotten anything about this man.

Maybe you ought to try to get in touch with him, Mike Mitchell had said. And later, *I wish I'd said everything I felt.*

Life and death. The terrible reality of both had been made brutally clear to her during the last few weeks.

She no longer had Mike's wedding ring or the dog tags he'd worn around his neck. Those had been taken from her by the women at Abdul Rahim's compound. Still, she had flown out to visit the pilot's widow and children yesterday.

She had shared with them the things Mike had told her. And when she had given Karen Mitchell the messages she'd been charged with, they had cried together.

As hard as that all had been, especially seeing his children and realizing that they would never know the father who had loved them so much, she knew that visit had helped. It had helped *both* of them. And Mike Mitchell's legacy was the sole reason she now held in trembling fingers the card Griff had slid across his desk.

Not everyone got a second chance. Win or lose, she owed it to the memory of the friend she had made, and so quickly lost, to find the courage to reach out for this one.

Only...not by phone, she decided, as her hand hovered over the receiver.

She needed to see that beautiful, lean face. To hear the emotion that underlay whatever words he'd say. To look into that single dark eye and try to read the thoughts that moved behind it. Then, and only then, would she know if what he told her was the truth.

"THERE'S SOMEONE HERE TO SEE you, Mr. James. I tried to explain—"

Irritated by the interruption, Landon looked up from the report he'd just received from an operative in Colombia. Grace and his secretary were standing side by side in the doorway to his office.

He got slowly to his feet, aware that the knot of anxiety, which had formed as soon as he'd seen the pale, perfect oval of her face, had quickly transformed into something else. Something that might certainly be classified as sexual.

It *was* sexual, he acknowledged. Just as what he'd felt every time he'd ever looked at Grace Chancellor had been sexual. Except now that familiar, aching tightness in his groin was accompanied by another, very different emotion. This one centered somewhere in the region of his heart.

She was dressed in a plain black dress, whose simple lines caressed the curves of her slender figure. Its severity emphasized the fair hair, which today had been pulled straight back from her face, revealing its purity of bone structure.

She hadn't lost the tan she'd acquired in Afghanistan. Nor had she regained the pounds the weeks of her captivity had burned off. And he had never seen anyone or anything more beautiful.

"It's all right, Sandra. Thank you." In his own ears his voice sounded strained.

His secretary arched her brows in surprise. Her head tilted questioningly, but after a moment she backed out of the office, closing the door behind her.

Leaving the two of them alone in a sunlit room high above the crowded streets of Manhattan.

"I understand from Griff that congratulations are in order," Grace said.

He couldn't read her tone, but it didn't matter. He knew well enough what she meant.

And although he wouldn't deny the pleasure he'd taken in Abdul Rahim's death, he had known almost as soon as it had been accomplished that it wasn't enough to change what he had become. Not nearly enough.

"Thank you."

"Thank *you,* Landon. I'm not sure I ever said that."

He smiled at her. "It really isn't necessary."

"It is to me. As empty as my life has been during the past few years, I discovered I wasn't ready to surrender it."

The same emotion he'd felt when he had looked up and found her standing in the doorway, a reaction similar to that adrenaline-driven burst of panic when a mission has suddenly—and unexpectedly—become perilous, surged through his chest once more.

As empty as my life has been...

It was a confession he might have made. If he had the courage to be as honest.

"So…" she went on, her fingers twisting the strap of the leather purse she carried, "I came to thank you for giving me back my life. Such as it is."

"Grace—"

"And to tell you that I went to see Mike Mitchell's

widow," she went on, speaking over his attempt to stop her. "I no longer had his ring, of course. Abdul Rahim's women took it. Still…I think she was glad I came. I was able to tell her about—" Her voice broke before she strengthened it to go on. "I think she was glad Mike wasn't alone at the end. I know *he* was. He was among friends, and he…knew that. Even in the short time I was with him, he taught me so much."

"I'm sorry they took the ring."

"It didn't matter. She has far more appropriate things to remember him by than a trinket like that."

He allowed the silence to build, realizing there was nothing he could say to that. "I hope you know I would never have willingly involved you with what was between Abdul Rahim and me."

"I know. Did you ever figure out how he learned you were back?"

"A disturbance in the Force?" he suggested, smiling at her again in an attempt to lighten the mood.

He found he wasn't ready to discuss Mitchell's death. Or Abdul Rahim's, either, for that matter. Not yet.

Grace shook her head, a small crease forming between her brows. She had probably been occupied in reading something deep and profound during the years he'd been imagining himself as Hans Solo.

"I don't understand."

"An old joke. The only logical explanation I can come up with is that Ahmad betrayed me. Maybe because they knew I'd trusted him in the past, they set it up so that if I ever contacted him again, he'd let them know. Maybe they blackmailed him. Threatened his family. Or

Reynolds may somehow have gotten the information to Abdul Rahim. Maybe he was busy verifying my identity during the days he held us. All it would have taken for anyone who knew my history was a description."

Unconsciously he raised his hand to the patch that covered the missing eye. When he realized what he'd done, he forced it down again.

"I'll probably never know for sure how the bastard knew I was there. Maybe he was as haunted by me as I was by him."

"Why would he be?"

"Because I was the one who got out alive. That isn't supposed to happen. Not in his world."

"When you escaped the first time," she clarified.

"I knew if I didn't, I was going to die a very prolonged and unpleasant death in that hellhole. Like you, I had discovered I didn't really want to."

She had been part of that discovery, although he wouldn't tell her that. He had believed at the time that if he could physically escape, he could leave behind what had been done to him. And asking Grace for another chance had been part of that hope. Only, nothing had worked out as he'd intended, least of all the ability to forget what had happened.

"Was it worth it?"

"Killing Abdul Rahim?"

She nodded.

"Let's just say that it was something I needed to do. Something I had needed to take care of for a long time."

"Griff said you could have gone back at any time."

"Maybe I needed an excuse."

Her expression changed. Before he could read whatever was now in her eyes, she looked down at her hands, still twisting the strap of her bag.

He wondered if he had again said too much. It seemed he was no longer able to mask his feelings as he once had. Not from Grace.

"And I provided that? 'An excuse.'"

"I would have come to find you, Gracie, even if Abdul Rahim hadn't been there. He was simply…a piece of unfinished business."

"And now that your business is finished…what about the rest?"

"The rest," he repeated cautiously.

"Mike Mitchell told me it's never too late. I hope he's right, because I want whatever you have left to give, Landon. I don't know whether I was wrong seven years ago about wanting it all. Or whether I'm smarter—or maybe just lonelier—now than I was then. But if there *is* any way we could go back…"

She had wanted a commitment. One he hadn't been able to make. Now she seemed to be telling him that she was asking for nothing.

Nothing but whatever he had left to give. The problem was he no longer knew what that was. All he knew…

"I love you, Grace. I always have."

"I know. I think I knew that then, but…I thought I had to have it all. Wedding and mortgage and babies. Those were all tied up in what I had envisioned as my life. All part of my grand plan. My mother used to say that to me."

"Say what?"

"That I had to have a plan. And I believed her. I've always had a plan. For school. For the Agency. Even for you."

He waited, knowing that she needed to tell him this, just as he had needed to tell her about Abdul Rahim. There would be time when she was through to answer the question she'd asked.

"I gave my life to the CIA," she continued, speaking more quickly now. "I worked like a dog, not only because I wanted to prove I was as good as the rest of them, but because I thought I was doing something important. Something good. Something that was necessary for the continued survival of this country."

And in exchange, they had kicked her in the teeth. Because she'd had integrity. Because she believed in the process.

"I've handed in my resignation. They'll think it's because of what happened in Afghanistan. In a way—a way they'll never understand—they'll be right. But…it has far more to do with Mike Mitchell and with you than it does with being taken prisoner. Or being threatened with death. I truly *wasn't* afraid to die, Landon. But…I was very much afraid to die alone. I still am."

"Grace—"

"So I've come to see if there's any way we can fix what went wrong between us. And even if you tell me there isn't, I won't ever regret asking you to try. That's something else I learned from Mike. Something I don't ever intend to forget."

When she finished, he let the silence stretch between them, trying to think how to express what he wanted to tell her so there could be no misunderstandings. He had told her so much. More than he'd ever told anyone, but he knew now that it wasn't enough.

"If you're suggesting that we try to go back to who and what we were seven years ago…" he began and again saw her eyes change. The clear blue darkened, glazing with tears that she quickly controlled. "Then…I don't think that's possible."

She suddenly looked as if she'd taken a body blow, so he knew he was screwing this up…something that should be so simple.

"We aren't the same people we were back then," he hurried on, trying to get to the point before he hurt her any more. God knows, he'd hurt her enough. "I'm not sure we ever can be again."

"Landon—"

"In my case, Abdul Rahim destroyed the man I thought I was. And despite what I'd hoped, killing him didn't bring that man back to life. And you…you were going to show the boys you could play in their park and not get hurt. Well, they hurt you, Gracie. Maybe more than anyone else *I* understand how much, because I also know how deeply you cared about their opinions."

Her lips parted, but she closed them again over the protest she had been about to make. She nodded instead, the motion quick and decisive.

"So…we'll never be those people again, but whoever we are—and I'm not sure either of us knows much about that right now—we could try to find out together."

"All right," she said, the slightly tremulous breath she took belying the composure of her agreement.

"But if you're only doing this because you don't want to die alone or because you're afraid of...whatever it is you're afraid of—"

"I'm doing this because I love you, Landon James. I always have. I just thought that in order to be a success at that, I had to end up with it all. The brass ring. I know I don't need that now, but...I *do* need you. I always will."

"I don't think much of your bargain, Gracie. You could do much better, you know."

Her smile was almost tentative, but it was definitely a smile. "I told Mike you were a tough act to follow. I don't think, until I put that into words, I realized how true it was. You'd be surprised at how poorly I did in attempting to replace you."

"I don't think I want to hear about that."

"No. Neither do I. I used to think about it, though. Wondering who you were with. Wondering...a lot of things I shouldn't have."

"Believe me, I wasn't any more successful at moving on. I knew how badly I'd screwed up, but I didn't know what to do about it. And then I went back to Afghanistan—"

"They say that sometimes when you glue the pieces of something that got broken back together, it's stronger than it was before. Do you suppose there could be any truth to that?"

He didn't. At least not with people. He had spent more than five years trying to put himself back together. And despite his success bringing Abdul Rahim to justice, he wasn't any stronger than he'd been before he'd gone back to Afghanistan.

"Maybe that's the wrong analogy."

"You have a better one?" she said, smiling at him.

"When they want to build the most powerful bows, they layer thin strips of wood, one on top of another. Each strip by itself could easily be broken, but combined... Combined they are virtually indestructible. Strong and flexible. Able to bend when they have to without breaking."

The analogy had given him some comfort through the years. The idea that strength wasn't totally about not bending.

Grace laughed. "Nice. And so obviously Freudian, as well."

"The imagery? Believe me, Gracie, there was nothing even *remotely* subconscious about that."

There hadn't been. He'd been thinking about making love to her almost from the moment Dalton had passed on Griff's offer. He still was.

"Don't call me that."

"Gracie? My darling Gracie. Whatever I call you, that's what you'll always be to me. I think you might as well just get used to it."

Epilogue

Grace realized at sometime during the very long night they had spent together that what she'd told Mike Mitchell had been true. Landon James was still a very tough act to follow.

Now that light from the rising sun was beginning to seep into the bedroom of Landon's Manhattan apartment, she could indulge in the forbidden pleasure of watching him while he slept. There were too many new scars on the hard, brown body. Marks whose origins she didn't even want to think about.

Only through the strongest act of will was she able to prevent her natural inclination to touch them with her lips. Or to trace gently across the roughened surfaces with the tips of her fingers.

She understood that that, too, would be forbidden. Just as the day when she'd reached toward the patch that hid his damaged eye.

Besides, touching those scars might awaken the man who had made love to her throughout the night. And that would destroy her opportunity to lie here, propped on her elbow so that her torso was slightly above his, enjoying the sight of his naked body gilded by the growing light of dawn.

She glanced up at his face, her gaze drawn by a subtle change in his breathing or by some movement she must have been aware of subliminally. She watched his eye open and then widen as it focused on her face.

"I thought I was dreaming," he said, his lips finally relaxing into a smile.

"I know."

The fact that they were again together, making love as if all those years had not intervened, had at times caught her by surprise. This morning she'd had the advantage of awakening before him. She had already had a chance to deal with the reality of their reunion. A wonder that had almost been lost in the intensity of their sexual response to one another.

Landon lifted one long, dark finger to run it along the fullness of her bottom lip. She opened her mouth, enclosing the tip of it.

"So beautiful," he said softly. "I'd honestly forgotten how beautiful you are."

She laughed, ducking her head a little. After a moment she lifted it again to meet his gaze. "You always did that."

"Did what?"

"Embarrassed me."

"How does telling you that you're beautiful embarrass you?" With his thumb he followed the upward slant of her cheekbone, tucking a tendril of hair behind her ear.

"I suppose…because I've always had a certain image of myself. One that didn't include that kind of descriptive."

"It should."

She shook her head. "Analytical. Stubborn. Determined. Cold, even. But not beautiful."

"You listened to the wrong people growing up."

"Not the wrong people. And not just growing up. Just…everyone except you. You're the only person who ever told me that."

"I was the only one crazy enough to think he could melt the ice maiden."

And there was no denying that he had. Years ago and again last night.

Landon had quickly destroyed whatever vestiges of modesty or anxiety she might have had about making love after all this time. When he pulled her into his arms, the complete and utter rightness of being there again had overwhelmed her. Any inhibitions had disappeared immediately.

This was where she belonged. She had known it from the first time he'd touched her. She knew it all over again.

And this time she would make no demands. No requirements except that he make a place for her here as long as he could. And as for what came next—

Carpe diem, she told herself. Seize the day.

Which is what she hadn't done before. She'd been too busy wanting the promise of a future. A commitment he obviously had been unable to give.

Now all she wanted was this. Landon. Being together in the here and now.

"And then I discovered that we'd all been wrong," he continued, his fingers tracing along her collarbone. "There was no ice after all. There was only…"

"Only what?" she teased when the sentence trailed.

"You. This. Offered so freely it took my breath. And then suddenly you backed away. As if there was something wrong with what we had."

"There wasn't. I just…" She stopped, unwilling to allow that old refrain to taint the feelings they'd rediscovered.

"You wanted more," Landon finished for her.

If she were honest with herself, she still did. But that was a lesson she had finally learned. What she wanted now, she told herself fiercely, was whatever he could give. Judging by last night, that was quite a lot.

Enough?

It would be. She would make sure it would be.

She bent, putting her lips over his. For a moment he allowed their caress, meeting the light, almost tentative invasion of her tongue.

And then, being Landon, he took control. As he always had.

He rolled, carrying her with him so that she was lying on her back, his body over hers. He immediately positioned his knee between hers, opening her legs in preparation for his entry.

There were no preliminaries as there had been last night. No slow, deliberately tantalizing preparation of her body.

Over and over again he had taken her to the edge of fulfillment before he allowed the intensity he'd so carefully created to fade. Then he had begun anew, his patience infinite, as he brought her once more to the verge of orgasm.

She had lost count of the number of times he'd done that. All she knew was that eventually he had mounted an irresistible assault against her senses until she had climaxed over and over again, her body trembling with an ecstasy only he had ever been able to give her.

Now, rather than the studied courtship of last night, he drove into her with a strength that was almost frightening. It would have been frightening if this had been anyone other than Landon.

Last night had been the velvet glove. This… This was the fist of steel it had enclosed.

She gasped as his hips rocked into hers, each downward thrust more powerful than the last. He had never made love to her like this. He had always taken care to bring her to climax before he satisfied his own desires.

This time, however, the courtship of her body was not only suspended, it was replaced with a demand. A challenge to become something she had never before been. An equal partner in their lovemaking.

Unexpectedly, the sensations he had so patiently coaxed from her body last night began to build again. Heat centered at the point where their bodies joined, radiating outward into nerves and muscles. It coursed like molten gold through her bloodstream, melting her bones until she was ablaze with it. And with him.

When the first shuddering convulsion racked his frame, her body arched, unconsciously meeting the increased frenzy of his movements with her own. As she felt the hot jetting of his seed, her own response was instantaneous.

She fell over the dark edge that had loomed before

her so often last night. And this time she hadn't even known it was there until it was too late.

Consciousness spiraled away into that void composed only of sensation. For a long time she was aware of nothing but her own shimmering pleasure. Then— gradually—her other senses began to function.

First sound. The harshness of his breathing. And her own.

Then touch. The hair-roughened texture of his chest moving over her breasts as his frenzy began to ease.

And finally, taste and smell. The salt-sweet essence of his skin as she pressed parted lips against his shoulder. The taste of it, familiar still, despite the long years. Beloved.

"Sorry." His breath stirred over the damp hair that clung to the side of her neck.

"For what? Not for *this*."

"You always seemed… I don't know. Fragile. Too cerebral. Now…" He shook his head, its movement against hers. "I didn't mean to hurt you."

"You couldn't. Not like this. And I'm *not* fragile."

It was an image she'd fought all the years she'd spent with the Agency. One she had never before realized Landon, too, harbored.

"But you're *not* denying the other?" He had raised his head, looking down at her face in the half-light.

It took a few seconds to think what he meant. *Cerebral.*

She'd always been proud of that. She just didn't see what it had to do with this.

"No," she said, and watched his lips tilt in amusement.

"Good."

"You should do that more often."

"Make love to you?"

"Smile."

"I think now I will."

After a second or two she realized what a beautiful thing that was for him to say. And then, a split second later, what it implied.

"Then, this… At least this…"

"Yes," he said, bending to touch her forehead with his lips. "And whatever else you want."

"What does that mean?"

She really didn't know. They had talked about so many things, including promises she was determined not to ask for. Now, however, he seemed to be saying there was *nothing* she couldn't ask for.

"That I want you here. Every night. And every morning."

"To live here?"

"Here. Or wherever you like. As long as it's with me."

Almost the brass ring. And more than she had been willing to hope for.

"Why?"

"You know why. I've been telling you why all night."

More than enough. She had told herself that whatever he could give, it *would* be. Surely she couldn't still want the words, too.

She closed her mouth so the request for them couldn't escape her control. *Enough. More than enough.*

"You said you were afraid you'd die alone."

She nodded, unsure why he would bring that terrible

confession up now. It seemed to have no place in what they'd found. It *shouldn't* have a place here.

"That's *not* what I'm afraid of, Grace."

"I always thought you weren't afraid of anything," she said, smiling at him.

Her attempt at teasing fell flat. Whatever Landon intended to say, he was deadly serious about it.

"Maybe that was true at one time, but only because I didn't know enough to be afraid."

"Didn't know enough about what?"

"About me. About my own limits."

Abdul Rahim. He was talking about Abdul Rahim. And that bastard shouldn't have a place here, either.

"Everyone has that kind of limits."

"I didn't think I did. And you're right. That was arrogance. Believe me, I paid for it."

"This?"

With her thumb, she brushed across the band that held the patch in place. It was almost lost in the matching blackness of his hair.

He flinched from her touch. The movement was slight, but enough to break the contact between them.

And then, before she realized what he intended, he reached up and pulled the covering away from the empty socket.

Perhaps that was designed to shock her, but if so, it failed. The physical damage was less than she'd been imagining. Still…

She waited, her eyes holding on his. After a moment he broke that contact, too, turning his head to look toward the windows. Her gaze followed, realizing that the sun was fully up now, flooding the room with light.

"You'd have seen it eventually," he said, still not looking at her.

She refused to voice the platitudes he probably expected. What had been done to him was barbaric. There was no way she would try to lessen its impact.

"Is that what you were afraid of? Showing me this?"

She was proud of the lack of emotion in her voice. It sounded infinitely more composed than she felt.

"You said your life had been empty." His head was still turned toward the window.

"It has. But that was my own fault. I have no right to complain."

"So has mine." He turned, finally meeting her eyes.

What he'd just said made a mockery of all those nights she'd spent picturing him with someone else. Instead... Instead he'd been as alone as she.

"I didn't want that for you," she said. "I never intended it."

"*That's* what I fear, Grace. Not dying alone. *Living* alone. Living without you. I don't think I can do that anymore. I know I don't want to try."

"You don't have to," she said, leaning forward to kiss him.

"I'm not nearly as arrogant as I used to be, but... At one time you wanted something other than...this."

She waited, despite all her avowals, hoping he might say what she had wanted to hear for so long.

"Do you still?"

A test? To see how serious she was about what she'd

told him. Or was it possible he was simply asking for the truth.

I wish I'd said everything I felt...

If she denied what she felt, would Landon interpret that as a change in the way she viewed him? One that had been caused by the confession he'd made.

Either way was a risk. And she had never been a risk taker. Not like he was. Not like Griff and the others.

She was the analyst. The one who relied on logic, not emotion. The one who weighed all the choices and then chose the safest.

Except, this time not taking the chance he was offering seemed the greatest risk of all. One she couldn't afford.

"Gracie?"

"I want everything. I want it all."

The brass ring. A marriage license. A mortgage. Babies. And all the precious things that went with them.

He took a breath, deep enough to be visible. Then he, too, leaned forward, resting his forehead against hers, as those long dark lashes hid the sudden glittering brilliance of his gaze.

When he leaned back, he was smiling. The same smile that had given her hope enough to begin this conversation.

"Marry me," he said softly.

"I thought you'd never ask." And that, too, was nothing less than the truth.

Maybe things work out as they are supposed to, she thought, as his lips closed over hers. Being called to testify. The assignment to Afghanistan. The crash. Being taken prisoner. Mike's death. Everything that had happened to her and Landon.

She had believed at the time those incidents represented the worst that had ever happened to her. And yet they had led, ultimately, to this.

She had no explanation for why that should be so. No possible reason for why, after she had decided that some dreams were not meant to be, she should finally be offered what she'd wanted for so long.

Having somebody to love you. Somebody you love in return. It's the only thing that matters.

Mike had been right about that, too. Maybe that was the answer as to why this was happening now. Because finally that was a lesson she had learned.

...the only thing that matters.

"I love you," she whispered. "I always have. I just didn't know how important that was."

"Neither of us knew. Maybe that's why it took us so long to find our way."

"And now that we have…"

"We've come too far to go back, Grace. I don't think we'll ever get lost again."

She nodded. Then she leaned forward, putting her lips against the empty socket. And this time he made no effort to avoid her touch.

* * * * *

Turn the page for
an exciting preview
of
RITA® Award winner
Gayle Wilson's
new novel of
romantic suspense
DOUBLE BLIND
coming in
November 2005

From HQN Books

CHAPTER ONE

CAIT MALONE threw off the covers, sitting up on the edge of the bed. She had already reached for the phone, when she pulled her hand back, taking another breath to calm her sense of panic.

The noise she'd heard could be anything. A raccoon in the garbage cans. A stray dog. Or, as she'd thought before, one of the neighbors having car trouble. After all, it was nearly daylight. There was no reason to panic and call 911. Not yet.

She put her left hand on the top of the bedside table, and then with her right, she eased open its single drawer. Her fingers closed around the cool metal of the semi-automatic she kept there.

Before she picked it up, the corners of her mouth tilted in a slight smile as she imagined her mother's reaction to the idea of her going out to confront an invader, gun in hand. Her mom wasn't the only one, of course, who would doubt her ability to defend herself. That she believed she could would probably come as a surprise to the people she had worked with in the Secret Service, as well.

Cait lifted her weapon out of the drawer, relishing its familiar heft as the SIG-Sauer settled into the palm of her hand. She knew from the comfort the feeling gave her that the hours she'd spent on the range during the last few weeks had accomplished exactly what she'd wanted.

Although her damaged arm had trembled with weakness the first time—after nearly two years—that she'd picked up her weapon, she had persevered until she could not only hold it steady on the target, but could regularly group her shots into the kill zone. Despite everything she'd been told about the extent of her injury, she had proven, to her own satisfaction at least, that protecting herself, if not others, wasn't beyond her capabilities.

Damn straight.

With the surge of adrenaline that mental affirmation gave, she stood up, stepping off the small braided rug and onto the coolness of the hardwood floor. Her bare feet made no sound as she tiptoed across to the open door of her bedroom.

Breathing suspended, she stopped to listen when she reached it. She thought briefly about turning on the hall light, but decided she didn't want to give whoever was outside any warning that she was awake.

Moving with a surety honed by familiarity, despite the darkness, she walked down the hall and into the main room of the small Craftsman bungalow she'd moved into and then gradually renovated more than six years ago. Almost unaware of the familiar ache in her shoulder, she held the gun with its muzzle pointed toward the floor, her left hand extended in front of her.

Exactly when she expected them to, her outstretched fingers touched the frame of the kitchen doorway. Even if they hadn't, she would have known where she was with the next step. The slate tile produced a measurably colder sensation under her feet than that of the wood.

Her fingers trailed along the countertop, following the line of cabinets toward the door that led out into the garage. She hesitated again when her hand encountered the knob of the pantry louvers, which meant she was within three or four feet of her destination.

Once more she paused to listen, again holding her breath. What she heard this time was definitely human in origin. A man's voice mumbled a profanity, accompanied by another of those thuds.

She leveled her weapon at the door to the garage, slipping her left hand under the right to hold it steady. At the same time she assumed the classic shooter's stance, she took a step back.

It was well and good to play Annie Oakley when she was shooting at paper targets. It was something quite different to face an assailant about whom she knew nothing. Not even if he was armed.

She had already turned, taking the first step toward the phone, when whoever was out there began to pound on the door. She responded automatically, swinging around to face it again.

"Cait?"

Her name. Spoken by a voice she would have known anywhere. Anytime. Under any circumstances.

She closed her eyes, slowly lowering the semiautomatic until it once more pointed downward. She could feel the sting of tears behind her lids, and she hated them. Hated herself for responding like this to just the sound of his voice.

She opened her eyes, blinking to clear the unwanted moisture. Of all the scenarios she had theorized to explain the sounds coming from her garage, she could never in a million years have contemplated this one. The confrontation that—despite all the battles she'd fought and won during the past two years—she was least equipped to handle.

"What are you doing here, Will?"

"Somebody set me up."

For a split second she thought he was talking about the recording the hotel security camera had made on that fateful night two years ago. The night before the assassination attempt during which she'd been wounded.

She quickly realized that didn't make sense. No one, not even Will himself, had ever suggested that what had happened had been anything other than what the official inquiry had determined. Faulty judgment exhibited by the senior agent in charge.

"What are you talking about?"

"Somebody murdered the guy I was working for. Only, they did it with my gun. Then the cops showed up and…"

"And what?" she demanded when he didn't go on.

"I need your help, Cait. I need…somebody I can trust."

Hitting below the belt, Shannon. Way below.

Quickly, before she could change her mind, she took the three or four steps that separated her from the outside door. In the darkness she fumbled for the chain lock. When she located it, she gripped its knob and slid it out of the slot.

Then she released the hold her teeth had taken on her bottom lip, drawing another steadying breath. With her left hand she turned the dead bolt, and with her right she gripped the knob. Finally she stepped back, bringing the door with her.

"What the hell do you think—"

Instead of answering, Will stepped inside, brushing by her so closely that she flinched from the contact. The knob was pulled from her hand as he closed and re-locked the door.

She could see little beyond the white dress shirt he was wearing, but he was close enough that she could hear him breathing—small irregular inhalations as if he'd been running. She took a step to his side, flicking the switch beside the back door. The overhead fluorescent sputtered on, flooding the kitchen with light.

Squinting against its brightness, she looked back at Will. He had lowered his head, shielding his eyes with his left hand.

"What's wrong?"

"I'm okay. I just need…"

She was almost unaware he hadn't finished the sentence. Her eyes had adjusted enough by now to take in the details of his appearance. The blood-soaked sleeve of his shirt. The fact that every stitch of clothing he wore was wet and that he was visibly trembling like someone suffering a chill.

Even as she watched, his body began to sag. Then, almost in slow motion, he slid down the door to end up sitting on the floor in front of it, long legs stretched out before him.

"What happened?" she asked, automatically stooping beside him.

"I told you." He didn't bother to open his eyes, his head against the door behind him. "The cops showed up. I wasn't in any condition to talk to them. And I knew what they'd think, so…I got out. Just not quite fast enough."

She used to know intuitively what Will meant, even when he talked in this kind of verbal shorthand. He'd told her once that he loved her because he never had to explain anything to her.

He loved her…

She didn't expect that memory to hurt as much as it did. She thought she'd dealt with these feelings a long time ago. After all, her relationship with Will Shannon was one of the first things she'd *had* to deal with after she was shot. And now…

"You took a bullet." Her intonation was flat. It hadn't been a question. Not with all that blood.

"And not even for the man." There had been a breath of laughter at the end, but it was quickly cut off.

"How bad?"

She reached out, intending to unbutton his cuff to push up the sleeve and evaluate the damage. She accomplished the first, but his sharp intake of breath as she tried to expose the wound made her realize that she couldn't do that without hurting him. She would have to tear or cut the fabric of his shirt away instead.

"I need to get some scissors."

Before she could complete the motion to stand, the

fingers of Will's left hand wrapped around her wrist. Surprised, she looked up, straight into his eyes.

They hadn't changed at all in the two years since she'd last seen him. They were the same deep chocolate that had mesmerized her from the day she'd met him.

"It's just a graze." His voice was thready. "Lots of blood, but obviously no arterial damage. And nothing's broken."

As if to demonstrate the accuracy of what he'd said, he tried to straighten his arm. This time his gasp was followed by a sighing release. Still, the arm *was* functional and, as he'd assured her, apparently not broken.

Some of her terror receded to be replaced by anger. The kind a mother feels after she retrieves her toddler from his dash into traffic.

"Why in the world would you run from the cops? Of all the idiotic—"

"I told you. I wasn't in any shape to explain what had happened. Hell," he said with that same short, unamused breath of laughter, "I didn't *know* what had happened. All I knew was that the guy I was supposed to be guarding had had his brains blown out with my gun."

I wasn't in any shape to explain what had happened…

"You'd been *drinking*?"

"No." His denial was quick. Satisfyingly decisive. Until he spoiled it. "At least…I don't think so."

"What does that mean?"

A long pause. This one she waited through.

"That I don't remember." He leaned back again, putting his head against the door and closing his eyes.

"You don't remember getting drunk?"

"I don't remember *anything*. Dinner." That was clearly an amendment to his first statement. "I was drinking club soda. I can't remember anything after that. I thought it would come back, but…" His head moved from side to side.

"So you *could* have been. You could have been drinking and blacked out."

"I can't remember the last time I had a drink. Maybe…six months ago. Maybe more."

"Things happen—"

"You can verify if I'm telling the truth." He opened his eyes to look at her again.

"How?"

"Smell my breath."

She laughed, but there was nothing remotely funny about the thought of getting that close to him.

"I'm not your personal Breathalyzer. If you want to take a breath test, you're going to have to call the cops. And if you haven't managed to destroy every brain cell you ever possessed, you'll do it right now."

"Somebody set me up to take the fall for a murder, Cait. My weapon was in his bed, shoved under the sheet in an attempt to hide it. I was unconscious on the floor. When I woke up, I was…I don't know. Disoriented. Uncoordinated."

"As in drunk."

His sigh was audible. Instead of arguing, however, he put his head against the door again. The small impact it made with the wood was audible.

She waited, thinking he would go on with what he'd been saying. Try to convince her. Do something.

When he didn't, she began to think about what *she* needed to do. Call the cops was first on the list, of course.

For some reason she didn't move. She continued to stoop beside Will Shannon, remembering things she hadn't allowed herself to think about in months.

Except sometimes late at night. Always at night.

"What do you want from me?"

It wasn't what she'd intended to say. But at some point in the midst of those memories, she had realized that no matter what Will might have done, she was going to help him.

Her decision would make no sense to anyone else. No more than his coming here would.

They were two people whose lives had been blown apart by circumstance. Now, it seemed, they had been brought back together by a situation just as fraught with danger—both physical and emotional—as the one that had torn them asunder....

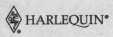

HARLEQUIN®

INTRIGUE®

What mysteries lie beyond the mist?

Don't miss the latest gripping romantic suspense in Rita Herron's popular Nighthawk Island series, coming in August 2005.

MYSTERIOUS CIRCUMSTANCES

A silent but deadly virus was infecting the residents of Savannah, Georgia, and FBI agent Craig Horn, with the help of Dr. Olivia Thornbird, was determined to find and eliminate the source. Then Olivia started feeling the virus's effects, and for the first time in his life Craig's professional goals become much more personal.

Available at your favorite retail outlet.

HARLEQUIN®

Live the emotion™

www.eHarlequin.com

HIMC

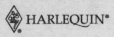 HARLEQUIN®

INTRIGUE®

As the summer comes to a close, things really begin to heat up as Harlequin Intrigue presents…

Big Sky Bounty Hunters: No man's a match for these Montana tough guys…but a woman's another story.

Don't miss this brand-new series from some of your favorite authors!

Available at your favorite retail outlet.